**When she finished putting the ganache on the rolls, she popped one onto a plate and handed it to Donovan. "Try this."**

He took an experimental bite, chewed thoroughly and looked up at her. "Heavenly. You put apples in the rolls. What's in the ganache? It tastes different."

"Unsweetened apple cider," she answered promptly. "Just a little to get the right taste." She slid a roll onto a plate for herself and then took a bite. "It's almost there. Maybe some candied walnut. Or…crystalized dates."

He nodded as he took another bite. "The adventurous eater would try the ones with dates, but the average eater isn't going to want dates on their cinnamon rolls, they'll just want butter."

"I agree butter is great, but people use too much of it, and it clouds the taste of their foods."

"That's how people are."

She didn't respond as she finished her roll. She licked the fork and found Donovan watching her.

"I like to eat," she said, "and I'm not going to apologize for it."

"I like women who eat."

"In your business, you should." She took his plate and put it in the sink, then opened the refrigerator to remove her bowl of chilled dough already formed into individual balls to start the crusts for her pies.

He reached over to touch her face. She remained still as he gently wiped a bit of ganache from the corner of her lip. Then he licked his finger. He smiled at her, and she tilted her head, walked closer to him and kissed him.

Dear Reader,

Jackie can't cook. But she can eat. Miriam sort of cooks, but really prefers restaurant dining with no dishes to clean afterward.

Regardless, food is an absolute necessity. We cannot exist without it, despite our love-hate relationship with it. Somewhere along the historical road regarding food, it has evolved into love. We gift people at various holidays and celebrations with cake, pies, donuts and other sweet concoctions to savor these important moments.

Food brings together two very different people in this story. Donovan Russell follows the rules. For him, food is about perfection. Hendrix breaks the rules. She puts together disparate flavors and makes them work. Join Hendrix and Donovan as they discover a passion for each other that is much, much better than chocolate.

Much love,

Jackie and Miriam

*J.M. Jeffries*

# BET ON *My* HEART

## J.M. Jeffries

**H HARLEQUIN**®KIMANI™ROMANCE

Recycling programs
for this product may
not exist in your area.

ISBN-13: 978-0-373-86398-3

Bet on My Heart

**HARLEQUIN**®
™ www.Harlequin.com

**Printed in U.S.A.**

**Jackie and Miriam** live in Southern California. When they aren't writing, Jackie is trying to take a nap and Miriam plays with her grandchildren. Jackie thought she wanted to be a lawyer until she met Miriam and decided to be a writer instead. Miriam always wanted to be a writer from her earliest childhood when she taught herself to read at age four. Both are avid readers and can usually be found with their noses in a book, or, now that it's the twenty-first century, their eReaders. Check out their blog at jmjeffries.com.

## Books by J.M. Jeffries

### Harlequin Kimani Romance

*Virgin Seductress*
*My Only Christmas Wish*
*California Christmas Dreams*
*Love Takes All*
*Love's Wager*
*Bet on My Heart*

Visit the Author Profile page at
Harlequin.com for more titles

**Jackie:** Thank you, Cheesecake Factory, for your Red Velvet White Chocolate cheesecake. With a little nudge, I can always get Miriam to have a planning session there.

**Miriam:** Thank you to Mars, Incorporated for white-chocolate M&M's. Jackie thinks she's enticing me to the Cheesecake Factory, but I'm just happy because I don't have to clean the kitchen. Also, a huge kiss to my newest grandson, Warrick Aurelian Pace, born August 2014. Big hugs to my granddaughter, Kathryn, who provides me with unending amusement. And a fist bump to my grandson, Frederik, who thinks he's getting too old for kisses. And to my children, you are both always in my heart.

# *Chapter 1*

Hendrix Beausolie took a deep, calming breath. *You can do this*, she told herself, clutching her tote with her pastry samples inside. She heard the crackle of the newspaper ad in her pocket. She needed this job.

The Casa de Mariposa had made a startling reincarnation in the past few months and was now being touted as one of the premier hotels and casinos in Reno. The hotel had buzzed with excitement from the moment she entered the lobby.

One last look in the mirror showed her makeup was still flawless, which was a bit shocking considering how seldom she wore it. Her black-and-white 1940s retro dress skimmed her curvy figure and her black hair was still carefully styled in neat victory curls around her face. *You can do this*, she mentally repeated her mantra. She practiced her speech one last time, took a deep breath and turned back to the restroom door. She yanked it open, stepped into the lobby and headed toward the restaurant.

The restaurant was busy with the lunch crowd. A good sign. She marched across the floor, through the door into the kitchen and stopped in panic. Aromatic smells of food cooking greeted her, as did the sounds of waitstaff shouting orders and the line cooks at their stations flipping sizzling steaks, tossing salad or standing in front of tables slicing and dicing. Controlled chaos.

"Watch yourself" came a voice from the side.

She stepped away from the doors to avoid a waitress with a tray balanced in the air on one hand. "I have an appointment…"

The waitress grinned. "All the way to the back at the very end of the kitchen and down the hall. First door on the left." She slipped through the door into the bustling restaurant.

Hendrix squared her shoulders and made her way to the back of the kitchen deftly avoiding people while muttering "coming through behind you." The corridor opened in front of her and she paused to gather herself. She took another deep breath, stepped up to the door the waitress had directed her to and knocked.

"Enter" came a deep, authoritative voice.

Hendrix pushed open the door and stepped into a large office with a kitchen composed of gleaming stainless-steel appliances on one side and on the other a desk set in front of rows of bookcases containing what looked to be every cookbook in the world. She had a hard time pulling her gaze away in order to focus on the man behind the desk.

He stood at her entrance with a half smile on his face. He was tall. Taller than she was, and she was five-ten. In the two-inch heels she wore, her eyes were almost level with his. He was good-looking with wide-spaced brown eyes and short-cropped hair. His white jacket was a startling contrast to his mocha-colored skin.

So this was Donovan Russell, chef extraordinaire, most recently living in Paris but now currently revamping the menus at all the hotel's restaurants located on the property. He'd been written up in *Reno Today*, an article Hendrix had studied for days, in an attempt to figure out what would impress him.

In person, he looked much younger than the photo accompanying the article. Maybe twenty-nine or thirty to her twenty-seven years of age. And Cordon Bleu trained. That part both impressed and intimidated her. She was totally in awe of anyone who had been trained in that mecca of French cuisine.

"I'm Hendrix Beausolie." She put her tote down on his desk and held out her hand ready to launch into her speech.

"Just show me what you have," he said interrupting her thoughts.

"I…" Startled by his brusqueness, she reached into her tote and brought out the container. She was deeply proud of her samples—a fruit tart, a couple of mini pies and her favorite cakes, including the champagne cake she'd developed for her best friend's wedding. She opened the container and lifted out a tray setting it down in front of him. Each tiny sample contained all the hope and love she had inside of her for creating delicious pastries. She bit the inside of her lip, awaiting his next move.

He stared at her offerings. "They look pretty."

"Pretty doesn't seem to impress you." She almost bit her tongue. She hadn't meant to say that. Why couldn't she just keep her mouth closed and nod. Her grandmother always said her smart remarks would get her in trouble one day. She hoped it wouldn't be today, but sometimes she couldn't stop the words from passing through her lips.

He stared at her, taking in her dress, her hair, and her face. "You're not a prima donna are you?"

"I thought about being a prima ballerina." She stood on point and smiled at him. "But I grew too tall."

He almost smiled. She could work with that.

"I don't need a baller—"

She picked up a morsel of champagne cake and pushed it gently in to his mouth. His eyes opened wide in surprise at her audacity, but he chewed. Then paused for a moment, his eyes studying her, and chewed again. Before he could say anything else, she popped a second piece into his mouth.

"Wow…" he said after he'd swallowed, but before he could go on, she popped a tiny fruit tart into his mouth. "I…"

"Don't talk," she said. "Just eat." She waited for

him to gulp down the tart. Before she could insert another one of her scrumptious little desserts into his mouth, he held up a hand, walked over to the refrigerator and took out a bottle of water.

Then he sat down at his desk and watched her expectantly. She laid out each morsel in front of him and indicated where he should start. Between each bite, he drank water to cleanse his palate. Hendrix sat down and watched his face transform from doubt to delight and finally to amazement. She wondered how many pastry chefs he'd already interviewed. She intended to be the last one. She needed this job.

"What's in this?" He said as the last bite of champagne cake filled his mouth. "I can taste the white chocolate and the champagne. What else?" His tone was still brusque, but he looked intrigued.

"A touch of raspberry, champagne, white chocolate and my secret ingredient." Her secret ingredient was a tiny amount of cinnamon and maple syrup. Her grandmother had told her the tastes would never mesh, but they did when added in the right amounts. She liked the lingering aftertaste of the cake.

"The tart," he said.

"Kiwi, pineapple, blueberries and raspberries with a bourbon and chocolate sauce." Her mouth went dry. She couldn't tell from the look of concentration on his face whether or not he liked it. She tried not to show how nervous she was. She'd learned to cook from her grandmother, and a childhood spent with globe-trotting parents had introduced her to the flavors of the whole world.

He leaned back in his chair and studied her. She gripped her hands tightly together to keep from shaking.

"Give me your background."

She wet her lips with her tongue. "My parents own an import-export business and I spent most of my childhood traveling and learning to eat different cuisines. I went to high school in San Francisco where my grandmother taught me to bring all the flavors together in her tea shop. I majored in chemistry in college and since then I've worked a number of places—most recently a bakery here in Reno and before that a restaurant in San Francisco and my grandmother's tea shop." Her grandmother's tea shop was named Hippie, Tea and Me. She usually avoided telling people that. Sure, her grandmother was an aging hippie, but her tea shop on Fisherman's Wharf was still in high demand. Usually standing-room only.

"Wait." He held up a hand. "Chemistry!"

She shrugged. "I like to blow things up." In her mind, food was a lot like chemistry with tastes that blew up when the right amounts were put together.

He burst out laughing. "I blew up my grandmother's kitchen trying to get a high school science project to work right."

"I blew up the dean's golf cart. I needed it for an experiment and…well…things happen." She raised her hands not adding that she'd almost been expelled until her parents replaced the golf cart with a luxury model and added a generous donation to the science department. She had the feeling her father was still chuckling about it.

He burst out laughing again. Then he frowned. "What did you say your name was?"

"Hendrix. Hendrix Beausolie."

He studied her for a long moment. "You're hired. You'll be in charge of the complete dessert menu for two restaurants, one a sit-down, dine-in and the other a diner in the lobby. When can you start?"

"Immediately," she said, relieved. She'd left her last job at Mitzi's Cake Magic rather abruptly. Even though she'd given him her references a week ago, she had the feeling he hadn't checked them. Should she be worried?

He nodded. "Report to Human Resources right away. I'll call them and let them know you're on your way. And be here tomorrow morning at four."

He mentioned a salary that made Hendrix gulp. She almost asked if he really meant to offer her so much money, double what Mitzi paid her, but clamped her mouth tight so it wouldn't get her into trouble.

She started packing up the uneaten pastries, but he stopped her with a wave of his hand. "Leave them."

She swallowed and nodded, unable to talk. She picked up her tote and fled. She briefly glanced back to see him digging in to what was left and chewing thoroughly as though trying to guess what was in each of her sample offerings.

Donovan had been bored. He'd interviewed several pastry chefs and not one had shown him anything interesting. Until Hendrix walked in looking sassy and just plain different. He didn't know what he'd expected from her, but she'd blown him away.

Donovan ate every last sample left on the little tray, even using his finger to lick up the crumbs. *Oh, my God*, he thought. He didn't know what was better, Hendrix or her cake. He could identify the main ingredients, but the subtle, pleasant aftertastes were harder. She'd used more than just bourbon and chocolate in the tart's sauce. And the tiny pie, which he thought was mainly key lime, had something else, some undertone that had a slightly spicy aftertaste yet was still completely and totally delicious. Better than any samples from previous interviewees and he'd interviewed too many to even keep count.

Just from the way Hendrix walked, he knew she was different with her odd black-and-white dress, black shoes and hair curled like she'd just stepped out of a poster from the 1940s. She was sexy, classy and had a look of fun in her amber-colored eyes. He liked her. He wasn't sure why, but that combination excited him. The way her food did.

Each one of Hendrix's samples had contained surprising undertones, and he knew she was never going to give him any more information on the ingredients she used other than the obvious. Yet her samples had been outstanding. Just thinking about them gave him a thrill.

And she was gorgeous. The sight of her heading into his office looking nervous and half terrified had rocked him. He'd gone into despair over the thought of finding just the right person to take over the pastry station after the last pastry chef had so unceremoniously quit. He'd wanted someone surprising and Hendrix was certainly that.

He sat back in his chair and stared thoughtfully at the empty tray. He'd been looking for unique and found it, though he already knew she would be a headache. Just from looking at her and eating her samples, he could tell she wasn't a team player. But if she could deliver quality every time, she'd really help put the restaurants on the map.

Donovan gazed around his combination office and kitchen. He was proud of it. Originally the office had been a small storage room, but he'd knocked out a wall and converted the expanded space into an industrial kitchen where he could experiment. He loved having his own private kitchen designed to his specifications. He loved every gleaming surface from the cabinets to the large worktable in the center with stools along one end so he could easily serve food when he and his brothers had a few food sessions on their guy nights. He'd even given cooking lessons to his new sister-in-law, Lydia, and his soon to be sister-in-law, Nina.

A knock sounded. He opened the door to find a portly man standing in the hallway. The man looked as though he'd just eaten a bowl of prunes. His mouth was pinched and his eyes were tired. He held up an ID wallet. Donovan tried not to groan. He'd been under scrutiny from the health department since his arrival.

"Come in," Donovan said. "How can I help you?"

The man glanced down at his tablet computer. "I'm Larry Deacon. I'm replacing your last health inspector. I'm just checking to make sure you're in compliance with the repairs you were ordered to make at the last inspection."

Donovan nodded. "I don't think I missed anything." The last inspection had been meticulous, with the inspector citing him over the most mundane things that had nothing to do with food handling, such as improperly storing dirty towels.

"I'll take a look around and meet you back here," Deacon said.

Donovan watched him return to the kitchen. Every time he had an inspection new violations were found. He would correct them, but sometimes he felt the health department was out to crucify him. He was pretty thick-skinned but at times the inspections seemed personal.

His phone rang and he pulled it out of his pocket. "Donovan Russell."

"Donovan," his ex-wife chirped. "How did you manage to keep the linen supplier on schedule? You never had a problem with him."

He tried not to groan. Even though he and Erica had been divorced for several years, she couldn't seem to get over no longer being married to him. "Erica, I always say please and thank you." Not that Erica was rude, but she definitely considered service personnel to be beneath her.

"Could you just call him for me?" she pleaded.

A former model, Erica had looks, drive and determination. What she didn't have was patience. "No."

"Donovan," she cried.

"We opened the restaurant six years ago. You know how everything works." Most of the everyday details had always been her job. And now that he'd sold her his half of the restaurant and moved to Reno, she called him over the most agonizingly silly things.

"But I don't have your touch." A tiny whine crept into her voice.

"Being polite is your first order of business." He closed his eyes trying to maintain his temper. After a couple of deep breaths, he was able to get beyond his irritation. "Erica, you need to hire a general manager to run the restaurant." A general manager would intercede for her and help keep everything running smoothly. "I gave you the names of people to call. Have you called anyone?"

She avoided his question. "You didn't need one." Erica's voice was soft and wheedling.

Donovan took another deep, calming breath. "But you do."

She drew her breath in sharply. "Donovan, can't you just come back to Paris? Your grandmother doesn't need you and I do. Nobody goes to a hotel to eat the food. And Reno is just a Podunk little town. It's not like Rome or New York or Paris."

He swallowed his irritation. "Erica, I'm not coming back to Paris. You can run the restaurant. I left you all the recipes. And you know how to cook." For someone who didn't eat, she was a darn good cook.

"Please, Donovan," she begged.

"No." He didn't understand why she thought she wasn't experienced enough to run a restaurant, or why she was so clingy. Her neediness was one of the reasons why they were no longer married. Her need to be admired, petted and supported had tired him out.

For an intelligent woman, Erica was kind of lazy. She always wanted other people to do everything for her. At first Donovan had been enchanted by her little-girl helplessness. But once they were married, her inability to care for herself got old pretty quick. He'd kept expecting her to grow up, but that never happened. They'd both been relieved to end their marriage after only a year.

He'd opened the restaurant, and her ability to be a charming hostess drew crowds. People returned because the food was outstanding, perfect in taste and presentation. Erica was the center of attention and loved it. The restaurant had been a success. She understood how to run it. He'd even explained everything patiently, writing out a schedule of what to order when and when to expect delivery. He thought she'd be fine on her own, but she wasn't.

"Erica, I have to go."

"Donovan," she cried, and burst into tears. "I don't know what to do. One of the line cooks quit and I need a new sous chef."

"I'll call François about the linen delivery," he said. "And I'll have Marie Odile Arceneau call you. She'll make a terrific general manager and you can go back to being the hostess." Erica hadn't made this much of a fuss when they'd divorced.

She stopped crying with not even a residual sniff. "You'll call him right away?"

"I'll call him right away."

She hung up without another word. She'd gotten what she'd wanted and was done with him. But he had the feeling that he would never completely be rid of her. He wanted to go forward and she wanted to go back. And to think he'd once thought her help-lessness charming.

The health inspector returned. "You have some changes you need to make, Mr. Russell." He handed him a list of violations. "You have a month to make corrections."

He took the papers and just stared at the list. One of the mixers was broken—again. Two temperature gauges in the refrigerators were missing and several first-aid kits were empty. A fire extinguisher wasn't properly seated in its cradle. One of the line cooks had improperly stored his utensils, which was something Donovan had warned him about repeatedly. And the deep-fryer station should be cleaner. "I will get on these immediately." He rubbed the bridge of his nose trying to release his irritation. All these violations added up to make him look careless.

Mr. Deacon's mouth grew even more pinched. "I'll be back in a month."

Donovan rubbed his eyes. He had too much work to do and not enough time.

"I'm disappointed in you, Mr. Russell," Deacon

said. "You're a first-rate chef and you know how a kitchen is supposed to operate. You have too many violations, and I can't help thinking someone doesn't like you. These violations aren't enough to shut you down and you still have an A rating, but I feel the need to warn you that these violations can't go on indefinitely."

Donovan had no answer. He'd come to the same conclusion himself, but that didn't mean he could ignore health regulations. He prided himself on himself on the cleanliness of his kitchen. He'd never had so many violations in his entire career. "I'll take care of everything."

"Fill up those first-aid kits. If I were you, I'd keep extra kits around just to replace the ones that seem to be losing their contents."

"Will do." Donovan watched the man leave and pulled himself to his feet. He opened the bottom drawer of his desk and dragged a bag out. He'd started keeping medical supplies on hand and had begun checking the first-aid kits every morning when he arrived. How the kits ended up empty, he didn't know. Even Scott, Donovan's older brother who specialized in security, was shaking his head over the mystery. He'd installed surveillance cameras that covered almost every inch of kitchen and still the mixers seemed to break when no one was nearby. Temperature gauges in the cold storage areas disappeared. He'd even found cleaning supplies near food prep areas, which was a huge violation.

He picked up his phone and dialed his brother to

let him know about the latest inspection and what it had revealed. Something had to be done. Eventually, the health department would get tired of these violations and shut him down. He couldn't let that happen.

## Chapter 2

"I got the job," Hendrix said to her grandmother, Olivia Prudhomme Beausolie. She cradled her phone against her shoulder while she sprinkled food into her fish tank. Her tiny little fish rushed to the surface to eat. She'd never been a cat or dog person. Animals had fur and fur traveled into every corner of a house. Her kitchen was immaculate.

She'd rented the cottage because the cheerful blue-and-white kitchen was huge while the rest of the cottage was tiny. The owner had liked to cook and knocked out a wall to create one large room from two smaller ones, doubling the size of the kitchen and then retrofitting the expansion with industrial appliances. The problem was that as a rental, the kitchen was a detraction unless the space was rented by someone who cooked and didn't mind the small living room and bedrooms at the front. That someone had been Hendrix after the cottage had stood empty for a number of months.

"A hotel!" Olivia said. "Why a big hotel? I thought you were happy with Mitzi Baxter. You had told me she and her bakery were wonderful."

"Mitzi's kids didn't like me. They thought I was going to take over and force them out." Mitzi Baxter had offered to sell half the bakery to Hendrix, but a stroke had seriously damaged her health and her daughters had taken over. Quitting had probably not been the smartest action, but Hendrix couldn't stand the way Lisa and Susan had hovered over her as though worried she'd steal a cup of flour and some raisins. "This way, I'm making double the money and can set something aside to open my own bakery." Opening her own bakery had been her original goal. Rows of cakes, pies and tarts filed through her mind. Someday, she promised herself.

"Sound's exciting," her grandmother said, though she sounded doubtful.

"It does, though I think he's going to be a little dictator. The executive chef is Cordon Bleu trained and you know how rigid they can be when you breathe around their food. Hopefully, as a pastry chef, our paths won't be crossing that much. He's even planning to give me my own kitchen so my desserts don't get contaminated by the odors in the main kitchen." Though for the moment, she'd be sharing his kitchen since he wouldn't have one ready for her just yet.

"That's good. He won't be standing over you. I know you work best when left alone." Her grandmother sounded amused. "I'm proud of you, Hendrix."

"Thank you." Hendrix grinned.

"Are you going to keep your experimenting to a minimal?" her grandmother asked.

Hendrix liked to dabble in the kitchen and see what she could come up with. The problem was, she often forgot what she did since she seldom wrote things down and too often couldn't reproduce what she'd done. "I plan to stick to my established recipes. I know them by heart, and I'll wait until I'm thoroughly certain he won't get upset before I start mixing things up." She tried to be more methodical about what she did, but too often she'd be caught up in the thought of the taste without paying attention to amounts. She liked having little surprises in her cakes. Her champagne cake had a very basic structure to which she added different ingredients in order to create more subtle tastes.

"Give your boss a chance to know you before you go creating things you can't duplicate," Olivia advised.

"I'll rein it in."

"Hendrix Marie Beausolie," her grandmother said with an undertone of amusement, "sometimes you just have to play along to get what you want."

True, Hendrix thought to herself, though she was shocked that her antiestablishment, unconventional grandmother would tell her that. Her grandmother had spent her life doing the unexpected and delighting in the fallout that followed.

Hendrix had to keep her goal of having her own bakery foremost in her mind. She would do anything for her dream.

They disconnected and Hendrix called her mother next. Her parents were world travelers searching for unique items for their import-export business. Currently, they were in Tanzania on a buying trip. She couldn't reach them, her call going straight to voice mail. She tried to calculate the time and figured her parents must be sleeping. She left a message telling them the good news. Her mother would get back to her when she had time.


The night manager had given her a white jacket and a toque with the hotel logo on them. She looked odd with the jacket fitting a touch too tightly over her bright yellow dress.

"I know I promised you a kitchen," he said, when he greeted her at the beginning of her shift, "but I don't have one ready just yet. I hope you don't mind sharing my office with me for a month or two while I'm getting yours ready."

"This is good," she said her eyes narrowing as she appraised the kitchen.

He was proud of the stainless-steel appliances, walk-in refrigerators with wheeled racks, industrial mixers and a worktable that looked to be ten feet long.

"The fire extinguisher holders are empty," she said.

Donovan sighed. He opened a closet, pulled out two boxes, opened them and hung the fire extinguishers where they belonged making a mental note to let Scott know that this had happened—again.

He then handed her a recipe box. "These are the recipes I want you to use. The ones in the last divider, I developed to appeal to people on a variety of different diets—they accommodate guests with allergies and diabetes and those on gluten-free diets. The ones in the front are more traditional dessert recipes."

"Okay," she said taking the box gingerly. "What about my recipes?"

"I want you to incorporate your recipes, as well." He opened the box to show her the neat sections of index cards inside. He pulled a few out and spread them over the surface of the work table.

Her lovely lips pursed. "But…but this is Reno. People don't come here to diet."

"People who come to Reno want safe fun. They don't want to die from a nut allergy because you used almond paste and didn't declare it. We want our guests to come back." *Alive*, he added silently.

"I suppose so," she said with a tiny frown.

He watched her turn his statement around in her head. Her face was as expressive as it was beautiful.

The casino was open twenty-four hours a day, which meant the kitchen was open twenty-four hours a day. The night crowds didn't eat as much as the day crowds, but they still wanted good food.

She twitched a bit, her shoulders rolling. She scratched at her long neck. Was she nervous? Donovan studied her closely. She didn't look particularly uncomfortable, but neither did she seem to be at ease.

He handed her a clipboard with the day's needs on it. She glanced at it.

Donovan watched her for a moment and decided she would be fine. He'd already shown her where the baking supplies were stored.

"I have some errands to run," he said. "If you need anything, here's my cell phone number. Just give me a call if you have any problems, or…if…you just need to talk."

She seemed surprised when he handed her a piece of paper with his cell number scrawled across it.

"Thank you," she said frowning slightly.

As he left, his last glimpse was of her standing in front of the huge table sorting through the recipes in the box with a slight frown on her face.

He headed to his car. He had an appointment with a rancher and then a butcher. As he opened the door, he paused. He'd given her his private cell phone number. No one had it except his family and the restaurant managers. Why did he do that?

He stepped out into the morning air. The sun was just cresting the horizon. The air was cool and crisp. He sat in his car for a moment.

To be honest, she was sort of cute and a little quirky. And she'd looked a little lost when she'd first shown up this morning. *She'll be fine*, he told himself as he started the car, backed out of his parking spot and drove out of the parking lot. *She'll be fine*.

For her first day on the job, Hendrix wore her bright yellow vintage 1950s dress fashioned after

one of Coco Chanel's classic chemise dresses. It was
her good-luck dress and she'd worn it for her first day
on every job since she'd found it in a hidden store a
block from her grandmother's tea shop.

Hendrix spread the cards out in front of her trying
not to wince. Boring. The recipes weren't bad, just
too conventional for her taste. Yet, her grandmother
had warned her to play along. Could she? Was the
compromise worth the job?

She sorted through the recipes, setting aside those
she thought had possibilities. Would he really notice
if she added something to give them an extra pop of
flavor? She flipped open her laptop to check out information on food allergies and then began adjusting the recipes to her own ideas of what they should
taste like without using ingredients that might cause
allergic reactions.

The jacket itched. She scratched at her shoulders. Maybe she should just make them the way he
preferred. And then when he liked her, and he was
going to like her, she could start flipping ingredients
around, nothing extreme. She wouldn't be outrageous.
She would play it safe. *Yeah, I can do that.*

She made a list of ingredients, pushed a wheeled
cart to the storage area and filled it with what she
needed to get started. Once back in the kitchen, she
started work despite the itching from the scratchy
jacket. She wanted her own jacket. This one didn't
fit right and she was going to be a hot mess by the
end of the day.

For the next few hours, she made cakes, rolled out

dough for pies, peeled fruit for fillings, made custard and crème brûlée. She filled the ovens with the aromatic smells of a dozen different pastries. On the side, she made cupcakes. Her special cupcakes filled with nuts, vanilla, cinnamon and a touch of ginger. She could do most things Donovan's way, but she needed one thing for herself.

The door opened and Donovan stepped into his office. A small, white-haired woman accompanied him. She had the look of an empress with her head held high, her brown eyes soft and mysterious and her tiny, slender figure elegantly dressed in a blue silk, formfitting sheath. The woman was so different from her own grandmother, Hendrix paused in rolling out the dough for another pie to stare.

The elderly woman approached. "You must be Hendrix. Donovan has done nothing but rave about your baking. When do we get to try something?"

"Hendrix, this is my grandmother," Donovan explained.

"Everyone calls me Miss E.," the tiny woman explained.

Hendrix watched as Miss E. eyed a nearby cupcake. Hendrix had been decorating them with white icing and little fondant butterflies. *Mariposa did mean butterfly, didn't it?* she thought. She would have to get a Spanish-English dictionary and check.

"Here." Hendrix thrust a cupcake at Miss E.

Miss E. grabbed the cupcake, peeled the paper wrapping away and bit down into it. A surprised look appeared on her face. "This is wonderful. Are they going to be on the menu today?"

"I don't know. I just wanted to cook up something that—" Hendrix caught herself in time "—that…was a little different." *A little unexpected*, she mentally added. She'd followed Donovan's directions, but the cakes and pies were dreadfully average. She'd resisted the desire to inject surprising ingredients to alter the flavors—almost. She couldn't help adding a little something extra to his apple-custard tarts and chocolate mousse.

"We discussed the menu," Donovan said with a sharp glance at Hendrix, who fidgeted, scratching at her wrists.

"Are you allergic to anything?" Hendrix asked Miss. E.

"No food allergies." Miss E. broke off a piece of the cupcake and handed it to him. "Try this."

As he popped it into his mouth, Hendrix thought about running away and hiding.

He chewed and frowned. He chewed a bit more. "This is good." His sharp glance took in Hendrix's face.

"I'm trying," Hendrix burst out. "I'm trying to cook the cakes and pies you wanted, but I can't. They're boring. They're too conventional. They're—" She clapped her hand over her mouth. "I'm sorry," she said in a little voice.

Donovan stared at her. "You can do better?"

Hendrix swallowed hard. Why couldn't she just stay silent for a change. "Your recipes are fine. I made them." She opened the refrigerator to show the pies and cakes cooling on different shelves. "Try one. You'll see." She started scratching again.

"You're scratching. Why?" Miss E. frowned at her.

"This jacket itches. It's driving me crazy."

Donovan frowned. "It's just a cotton jacket."

"It's not my cotton jacket." She bit the inside of her lip. "Mitzi always let me wear my own jacket."

"This is a perfectly acceptable jacket," Donovan said.

"It's not you. It's not the jacket. It's me. It throws my Zen off." Now he'd really think she was a nut job.

"Donovan," Miss E. said, resting her hand on her grandson's arm. "Leave her alone. If she wants to wear her jacket, let her. Who's going to know? She can wear a tutu and combat boots for all I care, I just need another cupcake"

Hendrix brightened. "Combat boots? Awesome."

"No combat boots," Donovan snarled at her.

She took an involuntary step back. "Fine, just my jacket…please. I'll leave the combat boots at home." Not that she had combat boots, but the idea was intriguing and Mitzi would have let her wear them if she'd insisted on it. She shrugged out of the jacket relieved to escape from the itching. She would bring her own jacket tomorrow—she cringed—assuming there was a tomorrow.

"Have you ever done a wedding cake?" Miss E. asked.

"I've done several different themes, wedding cake pops, wedding cupcakes and a seven-tiered marble cake." Weddings at casinos had become quite popular. *Did the hotel have one scheduled?*

"Scott, another of my grandsons, is getting married. When you have time, his bride-to-be, Nina, and I would like to discuss a wedding cake."

Hendrix grinned. "I love doing wedding cakes." Her champagne cake was perfect for a wedding. She could use pink champagne and decorate it with roses and daisies…her imagination began to soar. "I can cook up some samples for you try."

Miss E. grinned. "We'll be in touch."

Donovan's mouth was compressed in a hard line and he didn't look happy. Hendrix went back to her triple chocolate-nut brownies completely forgetting him as thoughts of how she would decorate the wedding cake floated through her mind.

"I don't think she's going to work out," Donovan said to his grandmother in the hall after he closed the door so Hendrix wouldn't hear. Not because of her cooking, but because she was too much of a distraction. He found himself thinking about her at odd times and he didn't like it. When he was in his kitchen, he needed to think about food, not some cute pastry chef and her cupcakes. Did he just think that? He did. She would have to go.

"She's going to be just fine."

"Grandma, it's my kitchen. You told me…"

"I know what I said, but if you don't keep that young woman around, I will be unhappy. People are going to eat here just to have one of those cupcakes."

Donovan glared at her helplessly. "But…"

"You used to be so experimental and creative in your own cooking. I let you have fun in my kitchen, even though sometimes I was cleaning goop off the ceiling at three in the morning. Maybe it's time you cleaned someone else's goop off the ceiling."

"Miss E…"

She held up her hand, her voice firm. "Just let's see how this works out."

"I'll be repeating those words to you when the kitchen catches fire."

Her eyes narrowed. "What's wrong, Donovan? You used to be so much more carefree in the kitchen."

"Guests have certain expectations," he replied. "They like conventional and don't like surprises."

"This hotel is about gambling. Everything else is gravy. If the extras can attract people, then the percentage that comes in for those cupcakes will also drop money in the slot machines. We're in the business of providing the fantasy, and food is as much a part of the fantasy as the gambling. When people feel special, they spend money. I want them to spend all their money here, not across town at some other casino."

"I'll keep her on a trial basis."

Miss E. patted him on the shoulder. "Of course you will. She's going to work out and she's going to surprise you in a way you'll never expect." With that parting shot, she stepped into the elevator and waved merrily as the doors closed.

He returned to his office, his thoughts a jumble.

Hendrix stood in the middle of the kitchen looking oddly hesitant.

Without preamble, he said, "My grandmother loves your cupcakes."

She nodded. "Awesome. But you're not so sure, are you?" She pointed at him, a spatula in her hand. "You're still on the fence about me. You think I'm weird, quirky and kooky."

"I try not to judge." Even to his own ears, he sounded defensive. Usually he was decisive and at times uncompromising when it came to food, but this woman put him off his game. The decision to hire Hendrix was either going to rock his world or blow up in his face.

"I know I'm a little unorthodox…"

"Is that the word you like to use?"

She smiled, a mischievous glint in her dark brown eyes. "No one has ever complained about the end result. I have a process and I know it's not always easy to understand. You have your own process. As much as we put spices, herbs and other ingredients into our food, we put our personality in, too."

She was shooting down every argument he could muster before the words left his mouth. "If you would give me a minute, I could express my concerns."

"Do you have any more?"

Defeated, he shrugged, "Not really."

She walked over and patted him on the arm. "That's how teachers teach chemistry in school. How to think logically and blow something up spectacularly."

"There will be no blowing up of anything in my kitchen. Ever."

She shrugged her elegant shoulders. "I'm cool with that."

"I hear you." He didn't quite believe her. He had the feeling his grandmother was right. He'd be cleaning gunk off the ceiling at three in the morning.

"You don't trust me yet, but you will." She turned back, walked over to the ovens and started opening them. Watching her move around the kitchen, it was almost as if she was dancing. There was joy in every movement as she pulled out pie after steaming pie and set them on the counter to cool.

The most amazing scents washed over Donovan. He knew without one shred of evidence she hadn't followed his directions as explicitly as he'd demanded. *Was that a look of guilt on her face?*

She disturbed him on a level he didn't understand. She was unsettling and unconventional. He didn't like feeling so out of control. This kitchen was his domain. He needed to get her into her own kitchen. That way if she didn't follow instructions, he wouldn't know. He would see the end result and wouldn't have to agonize on how she got there.

## Chapter 3

Hendrix walked out into the hot noon sun. Reno was so different from San Francisco, which was cool during the day and downright cold at night. Mark Twain had once said that the coldest winter he'd ever experienced was a summer spent in San Francisco. She missed the fog, the activity, even the culture. If Reno didn't work out she could always go back. But she didn't want to—she wanted to leave her mark here. This was her home now.

Having survived her first week with Donovan was a relief. She hadn't blown anything up or set fire to the kitchen. She decided she deserved a little treat. She climbed into her VW bug with the ladybug paint job, complete with eyelashes over the headlights. She headed for her favorite vintage fashion store after a quick stop at her house for some cupcakes she'd frozen for Hazel, the owner of Vintage Fashions. They'd be defrosted by the time she arrived.

Hazel Winston's vintage shop was a small store set in a tiny, out-of-the-way strip mall. She was a tall, curvy blonde with sparkling blue eyes and a penchant for vintage fashion. The store itself was small and felt cluttered with a dozen racks of clothes, shelves of vintage accessories and boxes of gently used shoes. On the walls, Hazel had hung lattice and there she kept her most recent acquisitions. She was an expert on fashion from the forties and fifties and her passion showed in the white tulle Balenciaga wedding gown that floated in ethereal splendor on the most prominent wall in the store.

Hendrix gazed longingly at the Balenciaga wedding gown, but the price was too steep. Plus, she'd first need a man in her life, and that wasn't part of the picture she had for her future.

Hazel dropped what she was doing and rushed over. She wore a pale yellow dress with a black-and-white polka dot neckline and cuffs—vintage Oleg Cassini.

"Did you bring my cupcakes?" Hazel demanded holding out a hand.

Hendrix handed over the box. "Hazel, do you have my dress?"

"I have three for you." Hazel placed the box on the counter and, after a small peek inside, she led the way to the back of the store. "Thank you for the cupcakes. They look wonderful."

"This is why I love you." Hendrix followed her. "You love my cupcakes."

"Everyone loves your cupcakes."

Hendrix had been supplying her friend with baked goods for a couple years. Part of Hazel's clientele came just for a quick snack while browsing the store.

Hazel grabbed the three dresses she'd found and hung each one over a hook on the wall. Hendrix was immediately drawn to a navy blue dress with embroidered yellow daisies on the halter top and a full skirt that flowed out over a white crinoline. She barely looked at the other two. One, a Dior form-fitting street dress of gray-and-green serge was almost as cute. The third dress was a black, pleated Coco Chanel silk dress with creamy white contrasting silk at the neck, cuffs and hem that would look heavenly on a romantic date.

"I'm celebrating my first week on my new job." She began to unbutton her yellow dress once she was in the dressing room.

"You didn't insult a customer or set fire to the kitchen, did you?"

Hendrix laughed. "I don't deal with customers anymore." *Just an annoying executive chef.* "I sort of miss talking to them." She didn't miss the complaints. No matter how good something was, one person would be dissatisfied. "And for your information, I only set fire to a stove once when I was adding butter rum to a chocolate sauce and some splashed over the rim of the pot."

Hazel laughed. "Where's the new job?" Hazel held out her hand for Hendrix's dress.

"Hotel de Mariposa," Hendrix answered as she pulled the navy blue halter dress over her head and settled it around her curves. The designers in the fifties really understood how to accent a woman's natural curves, which was one of the reasons she loved vintage fashion so much. She wasn't forced to slide her curves into current fashions designed for girls who looked like sticks.

"Ooh. The new *in* place. You are moving up in the world." Hazel helped Hendrix adjust the dress.

Hendrix stepped back to view herself in the full-length mirror clamped to the wall. *Nice.* A little nip at the waist and it would be perfect. She twisted and turned to see herself fully. "I'm going to wear this swing dancing next week. And I have just the right shoes for it." She'd found navy blue platform shoes in a sale bin at a resale store in San Francisco a couple years ago and she'd been saving them for just the right dress.

She wondered if Donovan did swing dancing. That would be a hoot, watching him trying to keep up with her doing the Lindy Hop or the jitterbug. She did a couple steps of the Lindy Hop and watched in satisfaction at the way the skirt flowed around her long legs in just the right wave action. This dress was perfect. She twisted her hips in a couple more moves and grinned at Hazel.

"I'll take it." She had room on her credit card and

with the new job she would be able to pay the card next month and still indulge herself.

Hazel helped her out of the dress and back into her own clothes. She fondled the dress as Hazel folded it and led her to the front of the store.

She walked out into the blazing Reno sun ready to take on the culinary world.

"The guests at table five are demanding to see the executive chef," the hostess, Rena Masters, said as she ran through the kitchen.

Donovan took off his apron and made his way through the kitchen and out into the restaurant to table five, wondering if they were complaining or complimenting. It was always a crapshoot.

"Are you the executive chef?" a woman demanded. She was in her early sixties with snow-white hair and a lovely face that owed its youthfulness to genetics rather than Botox. The man with her was distinguished-looking. He nodded politely after a smile.

"I'm Donovan Russell," Donovan said.

"I'm Lenore Abernathy. This is my husband, Bruce. You're apple custard tarts are divine. I've never had one so amazing before. How much do I have to pay you to get this recipe for my restaurant?"

Donovan reeled. The whole restaurant community knew who Lenore Abernathy was. Her restaurant, Piquant, was world famous. "It's a secret recipe."

She stared at him and he tried not to quake. "I would kill for your secret recipe."

Donovan was too stunned to think straight. "Um…"

How would he tell her that he had no idea what his new pastry chef had put in the tart?

"Donovan Russell," Bruce said. "I know your name. Don't you own Le Noir in Paris?"

"I did. I sold it to come to Reno and help my grandmother out."

Lenore nodded sagely. "I read about your grandmother. She won this place in a poker game."

"That's my grandmother."

"Bruce and I are on our annual food tour," Lenore explained. "And I need this recipe. I will be happy to call it the Russell tart."

"I don't know if I want to be a tart," Donovan said.

Lenore stared at him, eyes wide with surprise, and burst into laughter. "I do like a man with a sense of humor." She pointed at the empty chair across from her. "Sit down. Let's talk food."

Donovan couldn't refuse. She was authoritative, a bit too much like his grandmother. He couldn't say no to one of the most successful restaurateurs in the United States. He sat down and tried to figure out what he was going to say to her. He couldn't say he didn't know what Hendrix had added. And he couldn't just make something up and expect Lenore to be satisfied. She was astute, shrewd and a woman of substance. She would know he was lying.

"As you know, recipes are sacred," he began.

Her eyes narrowed. "Piquant is not only known for its dinners, but its desserts. And my clientele also buys my upscale frozen foods. I want to try this out in my restaurant. Who knows, it might make its way into the frozen food section of your favorite supermarket."

Donovan listened, thinking hard. His grandmother had told him food would bring people in. People came for the gambling and stayed for the extras. Having the tart featured at Piquant would also put the Mariposa on the map of food connoisseurs looking for the newest food experience.

He had two thoughts. First he had to sample the tart. Second he had to talk to Hendrix and find out what she did.

"I need to think about this and talk to my grandmother." And he should probably talk to a lawyer. He'd developed the basic recipe, but Hendrix had added to it, which he figured would make them co-owners. The whole idea was too confusing to think about at that moment.

"That's good enough," Lenore said. "My husband and I are leaving tomorrow, but we'll be back later in the summer. I will admit we love this hotel. The service is exceptional and the spa is to die for. Who knew I would find this gem in Reno? We'll be in touch."

Donovan knew when he'd been dismissed. He stood, thanked them both and retreated to the kitchen. He needed to talk to his grandmother, as well.

Having Lenore Abernathy want to add his dessert to her menu was an incredible opportunity. Yet, he was annoyed with Hendrix for doing exactly what he'd asked her not to do.

He grabbed an apple custard tart on his way through the kitchen. In his office, he sat at his desk and stared at it. The tart looked innocent enough and it was beautiful. Creamy custard bathed the apple slices arranged in a circle. A golden raisin anchored the center with two crescent shaped kiwis forming the leaves. The tart was a work of art. How had Hendrix found the time to do this? She was only one woman working the whole shift alone.

His brother Scott walked into his office, a half-eaten brownie in his hand. "Hey, bro. When did your dessert skills get so good? This is damn snacky." He held up a brownie.

"I can make a dessert."

Scott studied him. "What you can do with a steak is akin to Michelangelo painting the Sistine Chapel. But desserts? Not so much. Do not make me remind you of the 'what' cake."

Donovan almost shuddered. He remembered the "what" cake too clearly. The "what" cake was Donovan's first attempt to make a cake by himself when he was eight years old. Everything had gone according to the recipe, but when he took the cake out of the oven, the top layer looked more like a ramp than a perfectly domed cake. He tried to use icing to correct the slant, but the icing turned out too wet and kept sliding off. Miss E. wouldn't allow them to waste the cake and made them eat it. Donovan's oldest brother, Hunter looked at the cake and said, "what cake is that?"

"I've improved."

"Right." Scott just grinned.

Donovan grabbed the brownie and took a bite. The flavors practically exploded on his tongue. The brownie was a light yet dense chocolate extravaganza with undertones that made his mouth water. The basic recipe was his, but she'd added something to it. *What was the last bit of flavor? Maple! No, not maple. Caramel? Maybe.* And a touch of something else he couldn't identify. Damn, the brownie was good. More than good, decadent. More than decadent—it was food fit for the gods.

The woman could cook. First her tart was going to put him on the foodie radar and now her brownie was touched by hands of angels. If this was only a small indication of what Hendrix was capable of, he was going to have to live with her kookiness.

"I have to get two more to take home to Nina," Scott said.

"Nina is going to spin this, isn't she?"

"This brownie is going to be on a billboard."

Donovan could see the billboard in his mind and tried not to shudder. He did like his soon to be sister-in-law, but her mind never shut down. Donovan had already had one meeting with her in which she'd lain out her campaign to make the restaurants a five-star attraction. Nina was a bulldozer, jamming ideas at him every chance she got, making him want to run back to Paris.

His food had been the star of his restaurant in Paris. His reputation was his food. He wanted it to be the star of the casino, but Hendrix's desserts were eclipsing him. First, Lenore Abernathy and now Scott raved about the desserts but said nothing about the food. He would have to up his game. His food needed to outshine the desserts. How? He didn't know yet. His philosophy was all about slow and steady winning the race. When he developed a dish, he spent days thinking about it and weeks experimenting. His process was drawn out, painstaking and emotionally exhausting. And in one week, Hendrix, who just seemed to throw things together without thinking, had bested him.

Scott punched him on the arm. "Where did you just go in your head?"

"Thinking. Thinking…about…scallops." He wasn't certain he could tell his brother his ego had just gotten a big old kick in the butt. That would be unmanly.

"Really. Scallops. You didn't have a scallops look on your face."

Donovan frowned at his brother. Finally, he shrugged. "Since we're grown-ups, I'll confess. Hendrix Beausolie, the new pastry chef, made the brownies. And her desserts are better than my food and I don't I like it." His ego was definitely taking a huge hit.

Scott grinned. "That's my brother—always has to be the prettiest one at the dance, or no one is going to have any fun."

"I'm not going feel ashamed that my ego is dented. Maybe a little healthy competition is just what I need." In school, his instructors had told him he had a gift for food. He'd studied hard and worked hard developing his technique. To have another person with no formal training and a haphazard approach outshine him was just plain insulting. In Paris, he made it to the top in a city of outstanding chefs. Reno wasn't exactly the food Capitol of the world and he hardly expected to find any real competition. He'd accepted the challenge of building a dynasty with his family because he'd known, despite his reservations, that his grandmother was on to something.

Hunter and Scott thought Miss E.'s winning the Mariposa was a fluke. Donovan, being the youngest, had spent a lot of time studying his grandmother. He'd watched Miss E. manipulate them all into getting what she wanted. There would never be a middle-of-the-road goal for the Russell clan.

He'd watched his grandmother channel them all into the careers they'd entered once she'd figured out where their interests lay. Kenzie and Hunter were the artistic ones. Scott had had the potential to be either a cop or a master criminal, but Miss E. put him on the right road. And as for him, she'd known he enjoyed puttering with food and tastes. Even as a child, he loved to cook. She was a good cook herself, but her food was an expression of her love for her grandchildren, rather than just a skill set.

He wondered what food meant to Hendrix. Donovan got pleasure out of watching people eat his food and be transported by the combination of tastes and the artistic presentation. He suspected Hendrix wasn't interested in watching people eat, she wanted to play with tastes more to amuse herself than for accolades. And she liked to eat. He'd seen her dip a finger into batter and taste it. He'd also noticed how she made small samples for herself, which she also ate before she pronounced whatever cake or pie or tart she'd made good enough to be served to the public.

He had to find out what she was doing, how she was doing it and how to channel her technique so that it would benefit everyone. She'd bruised his ego, but his ego wasn't a fragile thing. Cooking wasn't for sissies. One of his teachers at the Cordon Bleu once told him, *to ensure success in this business you to have skin as thick as your ego is big*. And Donovan had a very thick skin.

# Chapter 4

Hendrix parked her car across the street from Mitzi's bakery. She sat for a moment deep breathing, trying to get up the courage to pick up her last paycheck all while avoiding Mitzi's two daughters.

Mitzi was only in her early seventies, and there was still a lot of life in her. Mitzi hadn't wanted to retire, but she'd had a ministroke and seen the writing on the wall. So Hendrix had made an offer to buy half the bakery and Mitzi had accepted. Mitzi made plans to do some traveling, but then she'd had a major stroke and lapsed into a coma. Lisa and Susie had promised they would keep the bakery on its feet, but then told Hendrix the buy-in deal was off because there was no physical contract to support her assertion that Mitzi wanted to sell her half the bakery. Hendrix had been furious. To have her dream within reach and then re-moved had left her ready to spit nails. Instead, she'd walked out and never returned.

She felt guilty for jumping ship. She owed Mitzi, but she couldn't stand Mitzi's daughters and knew her heart wouldn't be in her baking. And not loving her work would be worse than making crappy food.

Hendrix pushed open the door. The overhead blower, designed to keep flies out, activated.

The bakery wasn't large. Five small tables were arranged along the window in the front with the bak-ery case. The register and prep area took up almost the entire back half of the room. No one stood be-hind the register and Hendrix tried not to frown. Lisa and Susie should have known better than to leave the register untended. Mitzi had been robbed once by a man who'd simply reached over, pushed the open but-ton and grabbed the tray when the drawer slid open.

Besides the smell of yeasty baked goods, the added aroma of coffee filled the room. A couple of Mitzi's regulars sat at the tables. They all turned and looked at her.

"Hendrix," Josie Richland yelled. "Are you back? Please say you're back. Please, please, please." She folded her hands in prayer. Josie was a tall, slim woman in her midthirties with pale hair bleached almost white by the sun. Her skin was an attractive tan, testament to her many hours a week jogging so she could eat Hendrix's champagne cake.

Hendrix was too surprised to say anything. She just shook her head and stared at the other woman who ran across the old tile floor to fling her arms around Hendrix.

"What's wrong?" Hendrix said.

"The champagne cake sucks. The strudel is obnoxious and the cupcakes are like rocks. The only decent thing here is the coffee. Mitzi and you aren't here anymore, and the bakery is sliding into oblivion."

"I'm sorry."

"Please tell us where you've landed so we can change over. We've just been hanging around hoping to catch you."

"I came to get my last check," Hendrix explained. "Where is everyone?"

"Lisa is God knows where. Susie's probably in the alley smoking. Billy is in the back getting beans for a fresh batch of coffee. And don't worry—we were watching the register for him. I know you always said never to leave it unattended. Though I doubt there's much money in it." Josie looked sad.

Billy pushed through the double doors leading into the back carrying a bag of coffee. "Sorry it took so long. Lisa and Susie haven't ordered supplies for over a week. This is the last bag." He held up the coffee. His gaze lit up when he saw Hendrix. "Are you back? Cause if you aren't, you need to find a way to get me out of here."

Billy attended Reno Community College and studied restaurant management. Hendrix was never sure how he would get a job with his dark Goth look, tats and piercings, even if he did have charm and he was the best assistant baker she'd ever had. What that man could do with bread was what Miles Davis did with a trumpet. Sheer heavenly magic.

In the past week, her desserts were proving to be very popular, and eventually she would need an assistant. Billy would be great. He didn't complain about the four-to-noon work hours or the hot ovens or even the occasional burns. As long as she worked around his school schedule, he was good to go.

She would talk to Donovan. "I'll see what I can do."

"Where do you work now?" Josie asked.

"At the Mariposa."

"I've heard they have this famous Parisian chef overseeing the restaurant."

"Yeah," Hendrix said, "with his big Paris ego." Should she have said that?.

Josie laughed. "Has he tried your champagne cake?"

"He has…"

"And that wasn't enough for him to put up with your…eccentricities."

"We're still learning to dance," Hendrix admitted.

"I thought I heard you out here," Lisa called out from the back. She pushed through the half doors that led to the baking area. Unlike her mother who was comfortably round and soft, Lisa was all thin, hard edges. Her salt-and-pepper hair was pulled back from a narrow face and her dark blue eyes glared at Hendrix suspiciously.

"I came for my check," Hendrix explained.

Lisa opened the register, pulled the drawer out of

the tray and took out an envelope. "Here's your check, but you need to tell us where all the recipes are before I give it to you. Especially the champagne cake. We can't find anything."

"You can't withhold my check." She snatched it out of Lisa's hand.

"If you walk out of this store without giving me the recipes, I'll cancel it before you can get to the bank."

Hendrix's eyes narrowed. "You realize that's against the law. And I have all these witnesses."

Josie gave Lisa a death stare and even Billy puffed up his chest preparing to go on the offensive.

Lisa seemed unimpressed. "So sue me."

She turned to leave. "Bye." She wasn't going to be intimidated by this woman.

Lisa grabbed her. "Where are the recipes? They belong to this bakery."

"The recipes belong to me. And you can get a champagne cake recipe off the internet if you need one."

Lisa's blue eyes tightened. "You developed them while you worked here, which means they belong to us."

"No. They're mine." Hendrix pointed to her head. "But they could have been yours if you'd taken my offer and let me buy half the bakery."

Fury filled Lisa's eyes. "Those recipes are mine." She turned and stomped toward the back.

Josie grinned. Billy looked as if he wanted to hide somewhere. He needed this job and he wasn't about to antagonize Lisa too much. Hendrix patted Billy's shoulder. "We'll be fine. I've only been there a week, but once I'm settled in, I'll see if I can get you a job in the restaurant."

Billy nodded and returned to making the coffee.

Josie looked around. "I kind of hate leaving this place. We had some good times here, but it appears to have turned into a hostile customer environment."

"You all need to come over to the Mariposa," Hendrix told the few people left in the bakery. "I'll cook you up something special. We have a cute little diner that serves the best hamburgers in town."

"We'll see you there," Josie said after giving Hendrix a hug.

A few of the other customers nodded.

Hendrix felt bad about the decline in the bakery. She'd put a lot of work into the place and loved it. With Mitzi unable to communicate, her two daughters had decided to keep it all. The bakery had made good money. But from the look of it now, it was barely breaking even.

She was angry and sad—sad for Mitzi and angry with her daughters. They had taken a successful business and scuttled it. Hendrix knew Lisa and Susie thought if they could get her recipes they could lure back customers. They didn't understand that the bakery was more than just cakes, doughnuts and pies—it was customers, atmosphere and soul. The food had been the heart and Mitzi had been the soul.

Hendrix wanted to visit Mitzi, but the daughters had first told the hospital and later the nursing home that she wasn't allowed in. That hurt. Mitzi was family the same way Hendrix's parents and grandmother were family.

Working at the hotel was more anonymous. She didn't interact with the customers. She did her job and went home keeping her dream of owning her own bakery alive. But that's not how she liked to work. She wanted to be part of something intimate and special. She loved baking for people, which was why she wanted her own place. She wanted something like her Grandma's tea shop.

She stepped out into the swelteringly hot afternoon, anxious to get home. An idea for a mango cream pie circled in her mind, and she wanted to try it out right away.

She pulled into her driveway surprised to find a strange car parked in front of her home. She was even more surprised to find Donovan sitting on her front porch in the scorching heat. Her heart started racing and she wondered what he wanted. That man didn't even sweat and he smelled so delicious. It bothered her that she liked finding him waiting for her at her house.

"What is that?" he asked pointing at her car. "It's painted like a ladybug."

"How else would a VW bug be painted?" She glanced back at her car. The moment she'd seen the red ladybug VW sitting on the used car lot, she'd known she had to have it. It suited her personality so perfectly, she bought it on the spot. Even though she'd had to spend a large amount having the engine rebuilt. She turned back to Donovan. "You didn't come here to ask me about my car. Can I help you with something?" She opened the front door and cool air greeted her.

He held out a brownie as he followed her into the dark living room. "What did you do to my brownie recipe?"

*Oops!* He'd found out. She tackled her answer while leading the way down the long narrow hall to her bright, oversize kitchen.

"Wow," Donovan said, "what a nice kitchen."

"That's why I rented the house." She hung her purse and keys on a hook behind the pantry door. "The previous owner liked to cook. She upgraded the kitchen and knocked out a wall to make it a huge room. Unfortunately, the upgrade didn't match the rest of the cottage and she had a hard time selling it. So she turned it into a rental and I found it," Hendrix said, pleased that she had.

"Why do you have pink flamingoes in the kitchen?" He stared at an assortment of flamingoes leaning against the wall.

"The rental agent won't let me put them in the front yard. He said they were tacky." She shrugged into an white apron with flamingoes embroidered on it and started pulling the ingredients she'd need for the mango pie—butter, flour, cream, sugar and a fresh mango. "What do you want to know about the brownies?"

"Why did you change in my recipe?" His voice was harsh and angry.

He looked kind of cute when he was angry. She

tilted her head to watch him. He pushed the brownie at her and she bit into it. She chewed letting the flavors mingle on her tongue. "A touch of bourbon and sea salt caramel."

"Bourbon. Do you put bourbon in everything?"

"No. Sometimes I use butter rum. And tequila's only good if you have something fruit based. I've used beer in some pies." She handed the brownie back to him.

He stared at it as though it were an alien artifact. "Why did you change the recipe after I asked you not to?"

Her shoulders slumped. Guilt flooded her, quickly replaced by frustration. "Honestly, I tried to follow your directions, but every recipe you gave me is so by the book, there's…" *There's no oomph.* "There's no…" She groped for the right word, but it eluded her. "What don't you like?"

"I…I…" His face twisted. And then he sighed. "It's the best brownie I've ever had." He slumped against the worktable in the center of the kitchen looking defeated.

"Then why are you here, in my home, all angry and in my face?" She stood with her hands on her hips, frowning at him. "You could have said something this morning."

"Because you have to understand the casino is about gambling, the hotel is about comfort and the food…the food…"

She held up a hand. "Stop. Don't lecture me about food."

His mouth fell open. "Uh…excuse me?"

She wanted to stamp her foot in frustration. How could she make him understand? "Food is why we get up in the morning. Food doesn't just feed our body, it nourishes our souls. Food should be surprising and unexpected. Food should be…should be…an experience like riding a roller coaster."

His lips moved, but nothing came out.

She held up her hands to forestall his interruption. "Are you getting ready to fire me?" She bunched her shoulders, resigned herself to hearing the words. Was one week on the job some sort of record?

He grabbed her by her arms and looked at her. "I can't believe I'm going to say this, but I'm going to take you off the leash. I'll deny it with my last breath, but I want people to come to the Mariposa for the food. I want them to come for the mouth-watering desserts. I want…" His voice trailed away.

She smiled. "Okay, done. Do you swing dance?" At least now she wouldn't feel guilty every time she modified one of his recipes.

He drew back startled. "No."

"Do you want to learn?" He'd be terrific at swing dancing with that long lean body and natural grace of his. She enjoyed watching him move. She wondered if he knew how beautiful he was to watch. Besides, he was wound a little tight and needed to loosen up. He took food way to seriously. Food should be fun and she was determined to show him how to throw a bit of nonsense into his world.

"I don't know. Should I want to learn?" He sounded skeptical.

She wasn't trying to talk him into how to rob a bank. "You should always be open to new things." Hendrix laughed at herself, she almost sounded like her mother trying to coax her into eating chocolate covered ants.

"I went cliff diving three years ago. I'm good for a few more years."

Hendrix shook her head. "Swing dancing won't break your neck."

He stared at her thoughtfully. "I thought you would admire me for doing something reckless."

"Swing dancing isn't reckless. It's fun, but you do sweat." She pointed a finger at him. "Friday night. The Orpheum Ballroom. Be there. Eight o'clock."

"Are you asking me on a date?" His eyes narrowed.

"I'm not asking you on a date. You're my boss—that would be inappropriate. I just think you need a little fun in your life."

He stared at her, mouth slightly open as though searching for words.

"Trust me. You'll love it." She shooed him away. "Now go. I need to think."

Donovan sat in his hot car not totally certain what just happened. Somehow he'd been manipulated and he wasn't certain how she'd done it. After all, he'd once lived with the master manipulator of all time—his grandmother.

Hendrix was slick. *Well played, Hendrix. Well played.* He started the car and headed back home.

He hadn't even had a chance to sit down at his desk before Nina Torres barged in holding a brownie.

"Where are you hiding this amazing pastry chef you hired?"

Donovan sighed. He had the feeling he'd be hearing those words a lot in the future.

He had no idea how Nina and Scott had gotten together. They worked as a couple, a fact that amazed Donovan. She was just so energetic, so high maintenance. So not the type of woman Scott generally dated and here he was engaged to her, their wedding only a few months off. Another brother down, caught in the throes of matrimony. Donovan felt so out of the loop. The three of them had always been close and now the two eldest had defected to marriage and commitment.

Donovan always thought of the three of them as the three musketeers, plus one, with Kenzie, their sister. He missed their childhood, the fun adventures they'd had and the mischief they could get into. Sometimes, being all grown up sucked. Hunter had finally married, Scott was about to be, which left Donovan the odd one out. He didn't consider his one year marriage to be anything important. Miss E. had known before even meeting Erica that the marriage wouldn't last, but Donovan had refused to listen.

"I want to know all about the person who masterfully crafted this brownie." She held it almost reverently.

"She'll be here at four tomorrow morning like she is five days a week."

"I can get up at four in the morning," Nina replied. "If I don't go to bed." She took a tiny bite. "This brownie is incredible. I want to sleep with this brownie. I want to have babies with this brownie."

"Nina, does Scott know you're so weird?"

"That's why he chose me. He needed weird in his life." She gave him a smug smile and went back to nibbling on the treat. "I have to get this to my dad. Do you have any brownies left so I can ship a care package?"

Nina's father, Manny Torres, owned a high-profile restaurant in Hollywood specializing in Brazilian food. Donovan had planned to eat there once, but had been sidetracked and never made it.

"I'll have Hendrix make up a special batch and ship it overnight."

"Do you think she'll do a cake for my wedding? Or maybe just make a wedding brownie. That would be cool and different. I could build my entire wedding around a brownie." She took a bite, her eyes closed, a look of total ecstasy on her face.

Donovan mentally rolled his eyes. "Miss E. already talked to her about it."

"Thank you." Nina finished the brownie and licked her fingers. "I can't wait to meet her. I'm going to make this brownie a star."

"What about me?" Should he feel jealous of a brownie?

Nina laughed. "You're already a star." Fueled by

the brownie, she flounced out with the same level of energy she'd had when she'd arrived.

Donovan sat back and closed his eyes. No one was raving about his food. He'd spent years perfecting his recipes. He'd spent months retraining the kitchen staff to cook the way he wanted them to cook. And in a week, one upstart woman had everything in chaos. He had a choice. He could either back away and continue on the path he'd set or he could shake things up a bit.

He grabbed the menus for the restaurant and the diner off the shelf behind his desk. He'd been working on calculating his profit margins. And now he was going to have to rework his figures, adjusting them for the new dessert menus, recalculating prices up a bit to take advantage of Hendrix's popularity. People would pay extra for her desserts. Then he would tackle the task of making his food at the restaurant more exciting and less continental.

He opened his food bible. Every dish he'd cooked in the past ten years had been written down at all stages of development along with comments by staff and customers during the experimentation stage. What they liked, what they didn't like. How certain spices and herbs changed the tastes and how the final product did after being officially served to the public.

He wanted his food to be the star. What could he do to create that? He paged through his bible trying to look at each of his favorite recipes critically. He thought about substitutions, flavors, herbs and spices. He tried to think like Hendrix and ended up with a headache.

Why did he feel so compelled to change his dishes? He stared at the bible knowing that deep down he wanted to impress Hendrix. He'd been watching her for a week now and saw the way she approached each dessert. Her face lit up while she was cooking and for some reason he wanted her to look at him the same way.

He didn't want to like her, but he did. Erica had been skin and bones, so thin she was almost emaciated. For someone who liked to cook, she never ate anything. Hendrix's curves told Donovan she loved food. And he liked her curves. He liked the soft lines of her face and the way her eyes grew large with appreciation after she ate a sample of something she'd just baked.

At first, he'd wanted to get her out of his kitchen and into her own, but he didn't anymore. He wanted to watch her cook, to see what she did to give her desserts that little extra surprise.

His thoughts turned to her invitation to go swing dancing. But he didn't know a thing about dancing. He opened his laptop and started researching swing dancing. He found videos highlighting certain steps. The gyrations made him dizzy. He didn't think he could do that. But he was going to try because this was step one in impressing Hendrix.

## Chapter 5

Donovan spent the remainder of the afternoon cooking dinner for his family. Doing the unexpected didn't come easily to him. He decided on spaghetti. The whole world loved spaghetti, but he decided to make five different sauces. Each sauce was dramatically different. At least he hoped so.

"What is that marvelous smell?" his grandmother said as she entered his suite. She sniffed and grinned. "You've been experimenting."

"I'm searching for new ways to make spaghetti interesting."

She gave him a knowing expression as he handed her a glass of cabernet. One of the unexpected delights of Miss E.'s new enterprise had been finding one of the best-stocked wine cellars on the West Coast. Jasper Biggins, the previous owner, liked his wine, and Donovan had found some treasures. "Where's Jasper? I thought he'd come along with you."

"He's in San Diego visiting friends. He'll be back in a couple days." Miss E. appeared radiant when she talked about Jasper. Donovan wondered if something was going on between the two of them. "So what is the big to-do about?"

"I need volunteers to sample some food and give an opinion." He was not about to reveal his self-made competition with Hendrix.

Her eyebrows rose. "You want my opinion. You haven't asked me for that since you were twelve."

"I'm starting a new phase in my career."

"Huh." She studied him, her gaze shrewd. "People are growing and changing right and left around here. I can barely keep up with it. Does this have anything to do with all the raving people have been doing about a certain someone's amazing, decadent desserts?"

Donovan hated when his grandmother was so on the mark. "It has more to do with reshaping my brand, as Nina always talks about."

"Right. How are you planning on rebranding yourself?"

"I don't know. I just need to do something new."

Miss E. studied him so thoroughly, for so long he started to squirm.

"Then I'm ready to help," she said with a meaningful smile.

A knock sounded at the door and he opened it to Hunter and Lydia. Maya, Lydia's daughter, bounced in. A second later Nina appeared with Scott in tow. The gang was all there except for Kenzie, who'd taken a quick trip to Seattle to check out a new fashion designer she wanted to showcase in one of her boutiques.

His family sat around the table laughing and talking. Nina had finally chosen a wedding gown. Lydia insisted they have the wedding and the reception at her home, which had the perfect gazebo and a beautiful infinity pool that lent itself to the wonderment of a wedding.

He stood in his kitchen gazing around in satisfaction. Even though he'd redone his office to include an industrial kitchen, he hadn't been satisfied with the kitchen in his suite. Over the past two months, he'd completely redesigned it to his specifications expanding the cooking area, adding industrial appliances and a large table to work at. Currently, he was filling bowls with the different sauces. He then placed them on the dining table and added a heaping bowl of noodles, crusty garlic bread and a large bowl of salad greens.

Maya wrinkled her nose at one of the sauces. "Does that have red peppers in it?"

"Yes," Donovan answered.

He could see she wanted to tell him that she didn't like red peppers, but a sharp glance from her mother stopped her. She shrugged but managed to still act in as polite a manner as a nine-year-old girl should.

He placed all the bowls in the center of the dining table surrounding the big bowl of spaghetti.

"We're the tasting committee," Hunter said forking spaghetti noodles onto his plate.

"I need unbiased opinions." Donovan's brothers were always willing to tell him their feelings about his food, which was usually why he seldom asked. They were both meat and potato eaters, and Donovan knew he wasn't cooking for a French palate anymore.

They all sat down to eat. For a while the conversation was on Nina and Scott's wedding and Donovan was relieved Hendrix wasn't the topic for a change.

"Did you make brownies for dessert?" Maya asked. "Because I really like those brownies Hendrix made and there weren't any left at the diner when I went in to ask."

Hunter coughed, trying not to laugh. Lydia looked embarrassed at her daughter's comment. Miss E. just grinned.

"No brownies. I made gelato in five different flavors." From the look on her face, Donovan wasn't going to appease her. Maya wanted brownies. "But I'll call down to the kitchen to see if they have any brownies left."

She smiled happily at him, nodding.

"What do you think?" Donovan asked after he cleared the table and everyone waited as he scooped gelato into round bowls.

"I like the meat sauce," Hunter said.

"But the garlic-butter sauce is so delicate," Nina said. "I really like that."

"I like everything," Miss E. chimed in.

Maya pointed at the plain red sauce Donovan

had made. He wasn't surprised. Some children just weren't willing to try new foods. He pretty much had the children's menus down pat—hot dogs, hamburgers, grilled cheese sandwiches and plain spaghetti. Scott weighed in on the white sauce and Lydia commented on the pesto. They were *so* not helpful.

"If this is really for the buffet," Miss E. said, "then use all these different sauces. Give people choices."

"That is what I would to do," Scott said. "If you're redefining the buffet, I think people will eat whatever you offer them. Spaghetti is spaghetti."

Donovan closed his eyes. He'd hoped for more definitive comments.

"Donovan, dear," Miss E. said kindly. "You look a little confused."

"I've been cooking for Paris for six years now, and I don't have a good grasp on what the American palate wants anymore. I need ideas."

Everyone started talking at once.

"Chicken enchiladas." Nina looked transported at the idea.

Maya wriggled in her chair. "Hot dogs."

"Jambalaya," Lydia chimed in.

"Steak," Hunter added.

"Steak and baked potatoes with lots of butter and sour cream," said Scott.

Donovan held his hands up. "Stop. Stop. Everybody stop." Asking his family for their opinions had not been a good idea. He'd thought that each person would give an orderly collection of feedback on each dish but they'd gone off in their own directions making him more confused than before. "Just stop."

"When you kids were still in grade school," Miss E. said, her voice loud enough to capture everyone's attention, "I volunteered at your school for lunch period. I'm sure all of you remember. Mrs. Bickley was in charge of the kitchen. She had a lot more autonomy over what to cook then. She used to observe what the kids weren't eating. Maybe that's what you need to do."

"How would I do that?" Donovan asked.

"Mrs. Bickley used to go through the trash every day after lunch to see what was not being eaten."

"You want me to go through the trash!" The idea stunned him.

"Yes," Miss E. said. "Go through the trash and find out what people aren't eating."

He stared at his grandmother. That was going to be a huge endeavor. He had a hard time visualizing himself in hip waders standing in piles of food.

"Hendrix would do it in a heartbeat," Miss E. said slyly.

Of course she would. Hendrix would do whatever it took to manage her resources. And if that meant searching the food bins, she'd do it without hesitation.

He glared at his grandmother.

"For the greater good." Miss E. added, grinning at him.

The argument raged in him throughout the rest of the evening. He stacked plates in the dishwasher, cleaned the pots and, long after his family left, he was still battling with himself.

But it was for the greater good. He would have to suck it up and be a trash picker.

Hendrix parked her car in the parking structure. She leaned wearily against the steering wheel before forcing herself out. She was tired this morning. She'd spent the night tossing and turning with so many ideas floating around her head. After her conversation with Donovan, sleep had been elusive.

She walked briskly to the hotel. Even at four in the morning the hotel and casino were lit up like Christmas trees. As she approached she saw the waste collection area behind the kitchen illuminated by towering lights. She stopped just outside the area and stared. *What the heck?*

Donovan Russell sat on a stool with a huge blue tarp spread out across the asphalt. He was with three other men who had trash bags duct taped to their legs with latex gloves on their hands and surgical masks over their mouths. The smell almost knocked her down.

She couldn't stop the grin from spreading across her face. "Dumpster-diving day. I did this at the bakery."

Donovan looked up, his face scrunched with irritation. "Why would you Dumpster dive?"

"Same reason you are. To find out what people weren't eating."

"What's not to like at a bakery?"

"The cannolis weren't sweet enough. The éclairs needed to be creamier, not custardy. The German chocolate cake didn't have enough chocolate and tasted too much like uncooked flour."

A look of relief crossed his face.

"What's wrong?" she asked.

"I'm relieved that I'm not spinning my wheels here."

"When I worked for my grandmother, all the homicide detectives would take their breaks at her shop. They used to talk about going through people's trash. They said everything you ever needed to know about someone was in their garbage."

"I'm disgusted that I'm fascinated by that fact." He opened a trash bag and tossed gooey strands of pasta into it.

"I know, right?" She nodded at him. "I resent the fact that I have to think about my trash beyond which bin I toss it in. If cops can go through your trash and learn so much about you, so can criminals. I started shredding every piece of paper I threw away. I own a paper shredder that the CIA would love."

He glanced at her, eyebrows raised. "You have something to hide?"

"Just because I'm paranoid, doesn't mean someone's not out to get me."

He grinned. "Interesting."

"I'm just saying."

He laughed. "You see the world in a very different way from me."

"It's a blessing and a curse." She started to turn

away, but turned back. "Have you had breakfast yet? I've been experimenting with cinnamon rolls and plan to make some this morning for the staff to try. Do you want some? I'll have them ready in a couple hours."

Donovan shook his head. "I don't think I'm going to eat for the next five days."

She laughed. "I'd be more worried if you found a dead body in there." She gestured at the Dumpster.

"Again, the way your brain works is sort of fascinating. And when you have a moment, I'd like to use you as a guinea pig."

"And feed me what?" She wasn't enthusiastic about the menu he'd chosen. The Casa de Mariposa wasn't Paris. "If you want to know what locals expect to eat in Reno, you need to go to the Reno Food and Wine Festival. It's in two weeks. You need to incorporate half of what Reno eats with half of what the Continental crowd eats. Find a happy middle between American cuisine and French cuisine. Nina did a terrific job promoting the restaurant. Now all you need to do is keep people coming back."

Donovan waved her off and she retreated from the smell and the too-bright lights. Once inside the kitchen she shared with Donovan, she settled down to making the day's desserts. By the time she'd measured the flour into the mixers, she noticed the fire extinguishers were missing. They'd also gone missing the day she'd started at the restaurant. What was going on? She also found a bottle of cleaning fluid on her food-prep table which was a big health department no-no. She searched the kitchen and finally found the fire extinguishers in a cabinet. And after putting away the bottle of cleaning fluid she scoured her worktable and went back to her cinnamon rolls.

She'd just pulled out her last batch of cinnamon rolls when Donovan walked in. Small droplets of water clung to his hair from his shower, and she hid a smile, remembering the image of him sitting on a stool surrounded by discarded food. He sat down at his desk, and placed a pad of paper in front of him.

"Here," she said, sliding a spatula under a cooled cinnamon roll. "You need to eat comfort food after your experience with the trash."

"No comment." He sat down, sniffed experimentally and grabbed a fork as though just discovering how hungry he was. He ate half the roll before he stopped to look at her as she waited expectantly. "This is...truly wonderful." He dug in again.

"Good. I just wanted to wash the smell of garbage out of your nose."

"It's working." He practically inhaled the rest of the roll and held up his plate for a second.

She obliged him and decided to have one herself. She served a roll onto a plate and sat down across from him.

"Dare I ask what's in here?"

"No," she responded with a smile. "A lady must have some secrets."

"So I have to marry you to get your secrets." His smile contained a tone of teasing mischief.

She leaned toward him, turning on the flirt just a little. "Yes."

"Yes to what. Marriage or secrets?"

"Yes," she repeated, trying for a mysterious tone.

He sighed. "I need some coffee." He stood and stretched.

Hendrix heard his back crack and she hoped he hadn't hurt himself bending over all that trash.

"So what did you learn?" she asked once she'd finished her roll.

He finished setting up the coffeemaker and leaned against the counter while the coffee dripped into the carafe. "People don't seem to like fish much."

"I love a good salmon or tilapia and eat it twice a week. I don't know why people don't like fish. I've eaten all over the world and Americans really like their beef. They may not eat as much beef as they used to, but when they do, they want it to be spectacular."

"You mentioned once before, that you've eaten all over the world."

"My parents travel a lot for their business. They own an import-export business. I traveled with them until I was fourteen. I learned to eat some of the most unusual foods. I ate fish eyes in China. Sheep guts in Scotland. Goat's milk in Africa. Puffins in Iceland. I ate tahini and couscous in Morocco. You name it, I've probably eaten it." She stopped for a second to think. "I wouldn't eat crickets or grasshoppers in China. I know they're a delicacy, but I just couldn't get past the idea or the crunch. I tried them one time before and I'm particularly happy I will never have to eat them again." Her parents had insisted she try everything. Just one bite. If she didn't like it, she didn't have to eat it.

"I don't see anyone wanting crickets or grasshoppers in this hotel," Donovan said. "You've had quite a life. You said you traveled until you were fourteen. What about school?"

"My mom homeschooled me. We had lots of time on planes and in taxis going from place to place. She made every moment count." Her mother and father loved traveling. No place in the world was too dangerous for them. She had fun parents. Not many children had the opportunities she'd had. She'd thrived, though she had to admit she'd been happy to settle down with her grandmother and later here, in Reno. She still wanted to travel, but not now while she was establishing herself. "My parents were a little surprised when I came to Reno, though."

Donovan's eyebrows went up. "Reno has its own highlights. I traveled a lot when I was in Europe trying different foods in different countries. Admittedly nothing as exotic as you."

"What was your favorite food?"

"Anything French, but my favorite is coq au vin. I was never a big beef eater as a kid. I could cook chicken a thousand and one ways."

"I can respect that," Hendrix replied.

"What's your favorite food?"

"Whatever I'm eating at the moment. I love desserts. The gooier and sweeter, the better." If she had a favorite it would be a sweet summer berry cream pie she'd had once at a tiny, hole-in-the wall restaurant in San Francisco. She'd never been quite able to duplicate it. And when she'd gone back to talk to the owners, the restaurant had closed and no one knew where they had retired to or she'd have hunted them down and made them talk. In a nice way, of course.

"Why food? What attracted you to cooking?" She asked curiously. Donovan had the kind of looks that could have landed him on the cover of *GQ*. But he'd chosen food and she wondered why.

"My grandma first realized I had a talent for cooking. She kept me in the kitchen and out of trouble. She kept my brothers, my sister and I so busy, we didn't know up from down most of the time. How she kept everything straight, I don't know, but she always knew exactly where we were at all times and where we were going next."

"She sounds like a general. My parents were more laid-back, more about experiencing life than regulating it." Her parents hadn't kept her on a tight leash, but like Miss E, they'd kept her busy. If she wasn't learning how to tell the difference between counterfeit luxury goods and the real thing, she was learning how to speak a new language. "I've played in the Lalique glass factory in France. I saw the master designers create the drawings and the molds. The glass blowers let me blow glass and watch the artisans use all the different techniques in creating their masterpieces. I had a lot of fun and I learned a ton about glass blowing." She still had a little vase that she'd blown herself and dropped into a mold of delicate floral designs. One of the other artisans had finished it for her because she'd had to leave, and when it arrived at her parents' San Francisco home, she'd known she would treasure it always. Her very own unique Lalique vase.

She had a number of little treasures. In Morocco she designed her own tile. In Japan she learned how to perform the tea ceremony and design her own kimono. But her favorite treasure was from India, where she'd carved and painted her own Ganesh statue. She still had her very own elephant god.

"I'm kind of wondering the same thing as your parents. Why Reno?" Donovan asked.

She paused the conversation to check her cinnamon rolls. She needed to start the next round of pies. She liked this kitchen—it felt right, but she needed a larger worktable and larger ovens. The demand for her desserts wasn't that high, yet. But the restaurant and the diner went through about fourteen cakes, seventeen pies, a couple dozen tarts, four pans of brownies and five dozen cookies a day. The spa went through four dozen cookies a day. She knew the demand would grow as the hotel became more popular.

"Why Reno?" she repeated as she lathered ganache on the cinnamon rolls. "Reno sounded interesting. Because big cities are just big. I wanted to experience something different." When she finished putting the ganache on the rolls, she popped one onto a plate and handed it to Donovan. "Try this."

He took an experimental bite, chewed thoroughly and looked up at her. "Heavenly. You put apples in the rolls. What's in the ganache? It tastes…different."

"Unsweetened apple cider," she answered promptly. "Just a little to get the right taste." She slid a roll onto a plate for herself and took a bite. "It's almost there. Maybe some candied walnut. Or...crystalized dates."

He nodded as he took another bite. "The adventurous eater would try the ones with dates, but the average eater isn't going to want dates on their cinnamon rolls, they just want butter."

"I agree butter is great, but people use too much butter and it clouds the taste of their foods."

"That's how people roll."

She didn't answer him as she finished her roll. She licked the fork and found Donovan watching her.

"I like to eat," she said, "and I'm not going to apologize for it."

"I like women who eat."

"In your business you should." She took his plate and put it in the sink, then opened the refrigerator to remove her bowl of chilled dough already formed into individual balls to start the crusts for her pies.

He reached over to touch her face. She started, but he gently wiped a bit of ganache from the corner of her lip. Then he licked his finger. He smiled at her and she tilted her head, walked straight up to him and kissed him.

He tasted of ganache and cinnamon. His breath held a hint of apple.

She drew back and he stared at her, then he reached for her and kissed her again.

## Chapter 6

"She kissed me," Donovan said, a little in awe that Hendrix took the initiative. "And I kissed her back."

Hunter grinned and Scott shook his head as he bounced the basketball to Donovan and he in turn, bounced it to Hunter. They went to the gym several times a week to do, as Miss E. called it, *man stuff.* Which really meant sweaty stuff. Donovan had to do something to keep in shape with all the food sampling he did.

"That's how it starts," Hunter said. "One kiss and you're hooked. Next thing you know, you're buying a ring and being forced to pick out a china pattern and wedding invitations."

"A smart man will simply agree to whatever china pattern his fiancée wants," Scott added. With his own wedding looming on the horizon, he was surely deep in the throes of wedding mania. Donovan felt sorry for him. Nina was a bundle of energy that never seemed to stop moving, yet Scott followed right along behind with a big dumb look on his face.

"I've already done the marriage thing," Donovan said. "The kiss didn't mean anything."

"Then why are we being unmanly and talking about it?" Scott asked.

"She is my employee and could sue me for sexual harassment."

Hunter laughed. "She's cute. She's a bit funky, but Maya loves the way she dresses and definitely loves her brownies."

"She's odd," Donovan said, "but really nice." And she liked to eat. That was a huge plus in her favor. "She and Kenzie bonded over eyeliner."

"Can two people really talk about eyeliner for twenty-five minutes?" Scott asked. He threw the ball into the hoop.

"What possesses parents to name a kid Hendrix?" Donovan mused as he stole the basketball from Hunter.

Hunter grabbed for the ball. "Her grandma is like some legendary hippie in the Bay area."

"I think it's interesting that her parents named her after Jimi Hendrix. I'd never name a kid that, but it's something you don't forget." Scott blocked Donovan's shot.

Hunter grabbed the rebound. "I met her grandmother once when I visited her shop. I had some friends who raved about it, and I wanted to see for myself."

"What's it like?" Donovan asked, hoping to get a sense of Hendrix's mindset.

"Hippie, Tea and Me is a really famous tea shop," Hunter said. "The news did a puff piece a few years back. So I'm assuming her parents are a bit Bohemian, too, which makes the name Hendrix seem pretty logical."

They moved up and down the court for a few moments. The echo of the basketball filled the small court.

Donovan admired his older brothers. They'd taught him to be a man. And not once during his childhood did they poke fun at his fascination with food. Hunter built things. Scott blew things up. And Donovan created food sensations. Food made people get out of bed in the morning.

Donovan showed his love for his family through his cooking. For Scott's sixteenth birthday, he'd made a cake shaped like a pistol. When Hunter turned eighteen, he'd shaped carrots and raw potatoes into Lincoln logs and built a log cabin. One year, he'd made little cupcakes with playing cards tucked into each one for Miss E. And for Kenzie's tenth birthday he'd shaped a cake around a Barbie doll and created a wedding dress out of buttercream frosting.

"I'm going swing dancing with her," Donovan suddenly announced during a silent pause.

"You have three left feet," Hunter said with an amused grin.

Scott burst out laughing.

"No, no, no, Scott. You do not have the right to laugh. I watched you take tango lessons so that you can dance with your bride." Donovan tossed the ball at him.

Scott tossed the ball at the hoop and hollered when it slid in. "Nina does not take no for an answer."

"What makes you think Hendrix does?" He couldn't even convince himself that he didn't like that she took control of things.

"Because she looks like so sweet and funky in her own way." Scott leaned against the wall, wiping sweat from his face.

Scott hit Donovan playfully on the back as they headed toward the door and the showers.

Donovan enjoyed being with his brothers. They had all slipped back into their easy friendship as though they'd never been apart for the last fifteen years. They'd only seen each other on occasion, usually a reunion for Miss E.'s birthday, but nothing permanent.

Coming together to support their grandmother in her endeavor had made him feel closer to his brothers and Kenzie. In the car headed back to the hotel, he wondered if they felt the same way.

Hunter nodded. "I didn't think Miss E. was in her right mind. I was ready to have her committed."

"Me, too," Scott admitted. "But I think she has something going here and I'm willing to help her build on it."

"I looked at last week's cash receipts. The amount

of money this place makes in a week is almost staggering, and this is just a small casino." Hunter swerved to avoid a bicyclist taking up a good portion of the road.

"And it brought us all back together again," Donovan mused. "It's a bit unmanly saying this, but I've missed you guys. I missed being a family."

Hunter nodded. "I have to admit the same thing. Maybe Miss E. isn't crazy."

Scott nodded. "She knows exactly what she's doing."

Donovan agreed. "I don't think this was about her getting the casino. I think this was about her bringing us all back together. She's always been a master manipulator."

Scott took out his phone. "How do you spell that?"

Donovan punched his brother on the arm. Hunter laughed as he turned into the parking lot of the hotel. He pulled his SUV into a space and turned to look at Donovan in the backseat. "Miss E. wants us to be a family again. Having us all over the world, with only phone calls to touch base, didn't suit her. She wanted us back together."

"So she could get us back under her thumb?" Donovan mused.

"But we're not," Scott said. "She's always been a long-leash parent. She's let us make our own mistakes, but the minute you made one she pulled that leash back in."

"Is she pulling our leashes now?" Donovan asked.

As the youngest boy, he'd chafed the most under Miss E.'s thumb.

"No," Hunter said. "She's creating a family, the way they used to be years ago when no one moved more than five miles from home and were all invested in the family business. She's seventy-eight years old, and how much longer do you think we're going to have her? I think it's time to give back and make these last years the best years of her life."

An odd feeling crept over Donovan. Miss E. had never seemed old. The thought of no longer having her around created a dark hole within him. But even he could see she'd slowed down over the past few years.

"She wants us settled," Donovan said interrupting the silence of the SUV. "But she wants us settled where she can keep an eye on us.

Hunter turned off the truck and heat immediately started to build inside the car. "She wants us settled— wife, house, children, white picket fence, dog—in that order."

Donovan opened the car door into the Reno sun and glanced around. Family had always meant a lot to Miss E. "Yeah, bro. You're the closest one to having that."

"Don't remind me," Hunter said with a laugh. "I had this cute little dachshund picked out for Maya and she decided she wanted a shelter dog instead. We ended up with a monster."

Donovan had already seen the monster. It was nearly as big as a small pony, but Maya was happy with her choice.

"And now," Hunter continued, "she announced the other day, she wants a baby sister and she wants her named Eleanor Grace after Miss E."

"Nothing wrong with that," Scott said with a grin as they headed toward the hotel.

"Yeah, but eventually we're going to have to tell her the baby is a boy."

Scott choked on his laughter. "So that's why you got the dog she wanted."

Hunter nodded as he pulled open the glass door leading to the lobby. "Do I look stupid? A friend once told me that happy wives make for happy lives. I think that goes for daughters, too."

Donovan slapped his brother on the back, delighted to know a new generation was on the way even though Hunter looked a little uncertain. "Way to go, bro. Have you told Miss E. *she's* really going to be a boy."

"No. She agrees with Maya and wants a girl, too," Hunter said, "so I'm thinking of buying the dachshund for her instead."

Donovan and Scott burst out laughing. "Nina already has Kong."

Donovan knew Scott wasn't thoroughly in love with the tiny creature, but Donovan thought the dog was cute.

He headed toward the elevators. He needed to change clothes before heading down to the kitchen.

Hendrix finished icing the last cake and set it to cool in the walk-in refrigerator. One side of the refrigerator held rolling racks with cooling pies, cakes, tarts and cookies. The other side contained drawers with the fruits and other supplies she used for her baking.

Back at the stove, she melted chocolate, vanilla flavoring and butter in a huge pan over medium heat and whipped it until it was smooth. All the while her mind went back and forth over the kiss she'd planted on Donovan and the way he'd kissed her back. Giving in to the impulse to kiss him had not been one of her most brilliant moves. It had been unprofessional. But…the kiss had been heavenly despite the fact Donovan wasn't the type of man she was usually attracted to. She liked fun, uncomplicated men and Donovan was hardly that. He had layers and layers which both intrigued and worried her. She never knew what he was thinking, except for the knowledge he was as obsessed with food as she was.

She shouldn't have kissed him, she thought as she measured flour into the chocolate mixture and folded it in. She'd originally planned on a simple brownie recipe, but it had evolved into s'mores. She poured the batter over the graham cracker mixture and set it in the oven to bake. While the s'mores baked, she sat down at Donovan's desk, chin cupped in her hand, the memory of his lips on hers refusing to go away.

How could she have been so stupid? She was still proving herself to him in the same way she sensed he was trying to prove himself. She liked that he challenged himself. Like her, he didn't settle for the obvious even though she'd thought him reluctant to experiment at first.

Lately, she'd been eating lunch in the main restaurant, trying the different dishes she knew were Donovan's creations. The tastes were a mixture of subtle and refined. Almost a little too refined for the American palate, which seemed to prefer a bolder, spicier taste. Not that Americans were unsophisticated in their food choices, just more a product of combined cultures that intermingled heavily.

By the time the brownies were done and cooling in the refrigerator, Hendrix was hungry. Her shift was over. The head chef would send someone to collect the desserts for the day to be divided between the buffet, the diner and the restaurant. She decided she'd go to lunch.

In the bathroom, she changed from her uniform of white jacket and pants to her street clothes—a vintage fifties red, black and white plaid dress with a full skirt, trimmed with a white collar and cuffs. She then headed through the main kitchen and out into the restaurant.

The restaurant was busy with the lunch crowd, but she spotted an empty booth in a corner where she could watch everyone eat without being obvious.

The hostess brought her a menu. "What's the dessert of the day?"

"S'mores," Hendrix replied. "They're cooling and will be available soon."

The hostess grinned. "Everybody loves your desserts. Your white chocolate éclairs were the hit yesterday."

"I'll remember that," Hendrix said. "I was experimenting." She'd added a hint of nutmeg to the white chocolate cream filling—just enough to tantalize a person's taste buds. The thought of the éclairs made her mouth water. She'd really enjoyed making them.

"You say that every day. When are you going to make champagne cake again?"

"I had an idea for a variation on it. I'm going to practice it tomorrow and if it works, I'll make them Friday morning." The weekends were always the heaviest dessert days. She put in overtime on Friday to get the weekend desserts completed. And Friday night was her date with Donovan. She's been a bit bold about that, too.

"Can't wait!"

Hendrix glanced over the menu. "What do the employees eat?"

"They don't eat in this restaurant very often. Usually the diner or the buffet." The waitress looked a little uncomfortable answering Hendrix's question. "Though the family eats here a lot. Miss E. really likes the tilapia, especially the sauce Mr. Donovan created just for the fish. I'll admit I like it a lot better, too. The old chef, what's-his-name, never asked anybody what they liked. Mr. Donovan does. He likes to check in to see what we're eating."

"I'm always curious about what people are eating. Especially dessert."

The hostess grinned. She leaned over the table. "That strudel you made last week was so buttery I took home the last one for my midnight snack. I loved the cherries and walnuts and that hint of something that I couldn't figure out."

"Rum," Hendrix supplied. "Butter rum. Helps with that buttery flavor."

"Between you and Mr. Donovan, I've gained five pounds in the past month. He's certainly made a difference. Before I used to have several complaints about the food each night. Now, I get maybe one a week."

"That's good to know, but you didn't answer my question about what the employees like to eat."

"They try everything," the hostess said. "The only ones who don't are the ones who are picky eaters to begin with or have certain allergies. Pam over in the diner has celiac disease. So she can't eat anything with gluten. Don who manages the buffet is allergic to peanuts. And customers have their own allergies, as well. I always try to let people know if there's peanuts in something."

"But what do the staff like?" Hendrix persisted. She glanced at the customers around the room. They all seemed to have something different on their plate.

"At the buffet, they like the shrimp. Here in this restaurant, the beef bourguignon is very popular. I don't know about the diner since that's just hamburgers and hotdogs, what I call family food for guests with children."

"Okay, that's interesting." Beef bourguignonne was a safe dish. Most people were familiar with the ingredients and the taste. The dish was considered simple but sophisticated, which told Hendrix that most of the employees didn't have an experimental palate.

"Most of us try everything so we can make recommendations," the hostess added. "But we don't always like everything."

"Thank you," Hendrix said. "I haven't tried the beef bourguignon. I'll have it for lunch today."

"You won't be disappointed."

Hendrix sat back and looked at the other lunch diners. Most of the guests had sandwiches and salads in front of them. After all, it was lunchtime. She had a lot to think about.

Donovan watched the busboy pull the first of several racks into the main kitchen. Every head in the kitchen turned to glance at Hendrix's offerings for the day. One of the waitresses licked her lips as the rack passed her, a look of pure heaven on her face.

"She makes good desserts," Mitch, one of the line cooks said. He was young and had only been working for the hotel for a few months and was eager to learn.

"But have you seen the size of her butt?" another line chef said caustically. "She probably eats more than she bakes."

Donovan's hackles rose. "Excuse me." The slightest slur against Hendrix sent him into defensive mode. She didn't deserve such mean-spirited comments.

The two line cooks glanced at him. Mitch had the grace to blush. "Sorry, Mr. Donovan."

"Your comments are in bad taste. I won't have it in my kitchen. Consider this a verbal warning."

Both men nodded. One slunk away and the other turned back to his station. Donovan continued on his way out of the kitchen into the dining room. He saw Hendrix sitting in the corner eating.

"Can I join you?" he asked.

She nodded. "Sure."

"What are you doing?" She wrote in a notebook as she ate.

"Making notes?"

He tilted his head trying to see what she was writing. The notebook was open at the halfway point and the pages before curled slightly to show they'd been used. "Making notes about what?"

"About food," she replied, her voice holding a touch of impatience. "About what people are eating and about what goes back uneaten. Interestingly enough, most of your employees are a little more adventurous in their food choices than the guests." She flipped back through her notebook. "I thought my observations would add to your Dumpster experience."

"In Paris, I used to set aside one day each month for my employees to try my new dishes. But it was a lot smaller than this. I couldn't possibly do it for the hotel and casino employees."

"Why not create a rotating group of twenty you could try out new dishes on?"

"That's a good idea. I just haven't had the time."

She nodded in understanding. She knew the vandalism and petty thefts worried him. He could only work on one problem at a time.

"How to you like the beef bourguignon?"

"I'm loving it, but there are no surprises."

He wasn't certain he liked her answer. "How do you want this dish to surprise you?"

"I don't know yet." Her eyes widened as she let out a long sigh. "I'll think on it."

Her face was so expressive. She didn't hold much back. He found that he liked knowing where he stood with her. "I suppose I could put a worm in it." He half jested.

"That's a surprise, but not what I had in mind." She grinned at him.

Her smile warmed him. "But it would wake up your taste buds."

"I've had worms. They aren't a surprise. They're a turn-off."

He shrugged. "You didn't like them?"

Hendrix cringed. "They were actually pretty taste-less. It was the idea that made me squirm. But I pride myself on the fact that I did try them even though I was only six years old."

Donovan tried not to laugh. "I know for myself food is comfort." He liked knowing when he opened up his favorite package of cookies, the taste would always be the same. He would feel the same emotions he did when he was six years old. People ate certain foods for certain reasons.

"For me, it's the wonder." Hendrix paged through her notebook. "I like that unknown taste that lingers long after you've finished eating."

He chuckled. "You probably spend hours trying to figure out what that taste is."

"Nope, the thought usually pops in my head that this dish needs something to deepen the aftertaste, to bring it to full bloom, to increase the sensual feel of it."

He wasn't expecting that answer. "I'm not disagreeing with you." His gaze lingered on her lips and the memory of their kiss suddenly flooded him. "But most people eat for comfort. You eat for the adventure."

"And I've had *plenty* of adventures." She twitched a little as though showing off her waist.

For a second, anger flooded him. "Stop that."

"Stop what?" She looked confused.

"Stop acting like you're fat. You're not fat." She had such pleasant curves his fingers itched to explore them.

Her head tilted as if she were trying to understand him. "You lost me. What are you talking about?"

"When you said 'plenty of adventures' you seemed to mean that the food you eat goes right to your hips." Her hips were fine—he liked that she had lush curves. They matched her luscious personality.

She burst out laughing. Her laughter rang out over the dining room and several heads turned to look at her. "I meant the adventure of discovery. My parents were in Vietnam buying silk and I found this marvelous hole-in-the-wall restaurant in Hanoi. It was down this horrible little alley, but I still found it. I couldn't speak one of word of Vietnamese and this little old man who did the cooking couldn't speak one word of English. But once he figured out I wanted to try his food, he made samples of everything, and I ate every morsel he brought to me. I didn't know what was in half of them but the adventure stayed with me. And the tastes. I was twelve years old then, and my parents thought I was lost or kidnapped. They were at the American embassy trying to convince the US Marines to search for me." She chuckled and her face grew soft with the strength of her memory.

His anger died away and he realized he was a touch jealous. She'd done all these things, explored most of the world and all he'd ever done was go to France because France was where a person went when they wanted to learn how to cook. He'd been deeply influenced by Julia Child. The first cookbook he studied had been *Mastering the Art of French Cooking*. He'd saved his allowance for six months in order to purchase that book. He still referred back to it when he wanted inspiration.

"You seem troubled. What's wrong?" Hendrix finished her food and slid the plate away, her gaze on his.

"You've had this great big adventure. You've seen more of the world in your short life span than 98 percent of the population sees in their entire life."

"Am I hearing envy in your voice?"

"Maybe a little," he admitted.

"Like you stayed home on the farm or something? You built a successful restaurant in Paris, probably the most food competitive city in the world."

"I never went any farther." And he should have. He'd traveled around Europe, not as an adventure, but as another tourist.

"Don't be jealous. My parents wanted me to experience everything I could. I loved it, but after a while I wanted to stay home and do nothing. Yes, I had adventures, and I will always cherish them. I love my parents no end, but I'm perfectly happy in Reno. It's quietly exciting. Before I moved in with my grandmother, I didn't know I could be friends with my neighbors, I didn't know I could have a best friend, and I discovered that being in one place is just as exciting as being everywhere. I have a car I love, and I'm thinking about buying a house. I'm pretty sure I want to stay in Reno."

The image of her VW painted like a ladybug sprang into his mind. Somehow that car personified her. "Someplace you can put your flamingos out in the front yard?"

She held out her arms. "Right where everyone can enjoy them as much as I do. I'm enjoying domesticity."

"Me, too," he replied. "I loved living in Paris, but I'm learning to love Reno. It's not as pedestrian as I thought it would be."

She rolled her eyes. "I'm sure the inhabitants of Reno appreciate that."

He laughed. "I sounded like a pretentious snob, didn't I?"

"A wee bit." She held her thumb and forefinger a half inch apart. "But I'll keep your secret."

He laughed with her. "Listen, about yesterday."

With her head slightly tilted, she watched him. "What about yesterday?"

"We…you know…"

"Kissed," she supplied.

"That can't happen again."

She studied him for a few seconds, then shrugged. "Okay." She slid out of the booth. "I'll see you tomorrow night then. You remember, swing dancing at the Orpheum. Wear comfortable shoes."

"I'll be there." He watched as she strode away, her hips swaying and he wondered if he'd done the right thing, because he really wanted to kiss her again.

## Chapter 7

The Orpheum Ballroom had started as a movie theater, but as theaters started growing in size and number of screens, the Orpheum had been left behind
with no purpose or future. The front still had a theater
marquee and ticket booth. Hendrix loved the 1950s
flavor of it. Inside the seats had been removed, though
a few had been left in the gallery for people to watch
the dancing. A dance floor had been installed to level
the slope of the floor.

Hendrix finished arranging her cupcakes, brownies and fruit tarts on the buffet table. A few dancers
were already eyeing her new variation on the champagne cake she'd worked on all afternoon.

"What did you bring?" a man asked. She didn't
know his name, but she'd danced with him a few

times. He looked dapper in his black zoot suit and red silk shirt. He also had a gold chain tethered to his suspenders.

"Try them all and let me know which one you like best," she teased as she headed to the front doors. She went outside to wait for Donovan on the sidewalk. She couldn't help wondering if he was coming or if he would be a no-show. She tried not to be nervous. She really wanted him to come.

Sally Morehead, the first friend Hendrix had made when she'd first moved to Reno, walked around the corner from the parking lot. "Hendrix, why are you waiting outside?"

"I'm waiting for a friend."

Sally's eyebrows went up. "You invited a friend?" She was a pixie of a woman, with long silky brown hair, cheerful brown eyes and an every-present smile on her face. All the guys loved dancing with her because she was easy to toss around in the aerial steps and back flips. Tonight she wore a pink poodle skirt and a white sweater with a pink scarf knotted around her neck. She had her hair pulled back into a pony tail and looked as though she was still sixteen even though Hendrix knew Sally was almost thirty.

"I sort of invited my boss," Hendrix replied.

Sally grinned. "Okay. Why?"

"The words just leaped out of my mouth."

"That happens to you a lot." Sally waved at one of their partners, John Corning. He waved back and then went inside. When he opened the door, music blasted out to the street.

"I try to control my words, but some things just have to be said."

"And you're always the person to say it," Sally said. "Love your pants."

Hendrix glanced down at the black-and-white striped Capri pants she wore with a white silk blouse with a deep V in the front. "Found them on the internet, from the Pin-Ups Sex Kitten line. Not vintage, but perfect for dancing." The outfit made her feel a little bit like the naughty sex-kitten Rizzo from *Grease*.

Sally nodded. Donovan pulled up in his car and lowered the window.

"Park around the corner," Hendrix said, pointing. He nodded and drove to the parking lot.

"That's your boss?" Sally said, admiration in her voice.

"That's him."

"I can see why you invited him. See you inside." Sally opened the door and stepped inside.

Donovan walked around the corner. He wore black jeans and a white polo shirt. He had come dressed comfortably and Hendrix was impressed. He was ready to dance.

"You came," she said.

"Of course. Wouldn't miss this for the world." He grinned at her and held out a hand while his eyes moved up and down taking in her outfit. From the look on his face, he approved.

She placed her hand in his, he opened the door and they entered the cool interior.

Music blasted from a sound system. The room was

large enough for every couple to have their own spot. Hendrix started tapping her foot. She loved swing dancing. Once of her grandmother's favorite clients had introduced Hendrix to swing dancing when she'd been in high school and she'd been hooked ever since.

While all the kids in her high school went to music concerts and attended wild parties, Hendrix had gone swing dancing. They'd thought she was weird. Hendrix hadn't cared what they thought, which made her seem even weirder. While her girlfriends agonized over the popular boys, angling for dates, Hendrix would shrug. She had her whole life in front of her—why settle? Half her friends had gotten married the day after graduation but by the time they were twenty-one, too many of they were divorced with babies on their hips.

"Wow!" Donovan said, his eyes on the dancing couples. "I've seen swing dancing, but it always seemed a little intimidating."

"I'm starting you on the bunny slopes."

"I skied the Alps."

"Is hurtling down inclines at breakneck speeds supposed to impress me?"

"You don't ski?"

"No. If I'm going to break a leg, I'm going to do it here, as close to a hospital as possible." She tugged him onto the floor. "Come on. I'm going to teach you the basics of the Lindy hop and you're going to love it."

"Back step, front step, triple step, step, step, triple step, step, step, front step, back step," Donovan chanted. Moving to the music was easy enough, remembering the steps was going to be a challenge.

Hendrix was a patient teacher. While he went over and over the moves for probably the thousandth time, she started adding little wiggles to the movement of her feet and pushing up the speed after he mastered each series of steps.

He was enjoying himself. He tripped, regained his footing and flowed right into the next step, almost without thinking.

"We're going to add a little spin here." Hendrix positioned his hands on her waist. "This is a rock step, triple step, half step, triple step, rock step." She showed him and he found his feet finally moving in harmony with her and following the tempo of the music. He wasn't as familiar with the music, but he could pick out the beats and recognized the tunes of Cab Callaway, Count Basie, Tommy Dorsey, Glenn Miller and the present day Brian Setzer. Some couples had gotten fancy with jumps and slides and women being whirled. He recognized the woman who'd been talking with Hendrix when he'd first arrived. Her dancing was wild and uninhibited. She was being flipped and twirled by a man in a black fifties zoot suit with his key chain bumping against his leg.

The music ended and Donovan was almost breathless.

"Want to sit one out?" Hendrix asked.

"Water," he gasped.

They made their way to the refreshment table and grabbed bottles of water. She found two seats in the gallery and they sat just as the music launched into another song.

Donovan was completely fascinated by the dancing. "The dancers seem to be doing different versions of the same thing."

"Let me educate you. There's East Coast swing, West Coast swing, jive, Cajun swing, Carolina shag, imperial swing and about a half dozen more variations," Hendrix explained.

"What kind of dance are you teaching me?"

"East Coast Swing. It's a simple, six count variation on the Lindy Hop."

"What did you learn?"

"West Coast swing, but as you go along you pick up other things." She leaned forward to watch her friend gyrate through a particularly complicated series of steps. Her foot tapped in tune with the beat of the music and her body seemed to vibrate.

Seeing this new side of Hendrix was fun. He knew what a fifties girl she was at heart with her fashionable pants and white blouse. She'd pulled her hair back into a wild-looking pony tail that swung back and forth as she moved. He could picture her in the 1920s jiving to the music at the Savoy Ballroom in Harlem.

He could almost imagine himself there with her. His imagination took hold and he finished his water and stood up. He held out a hand. "I know I'm not at the caliber of your usual partners, but I'm having fun."

She jumped to her feet. "Of course you are. Did you think I would lead you astray?"

He laughed. "I'm hungry. Let's check out the buffet." He was always curious about food. He led Hendrix to the tables arranged alongside one wall at the back of the gallery.

He picked up a cupcake and set it on a paper plate. The cupcakes were glazed with a single half strawberry resting on the peaks. Hendrix gave him a nervous glance. "What?" he asked then looked down at the cupcake. "You made the cupcakes, didn't you?"

She nodded.

He took an experimental bite, and with eyebrows raised in surprise, he said, "Wow! Why aren't you serving these at the hotel?"

"I just kind of worked out the taste this afternoon."

He rolled the flavorful cake around his tongue trying to figure out what the underlying taste was. "Orange peel?" He took another bite. "Cinnamon?"

"And licorice root," she added.

"I can see how that would enhance the flavors." He finished the cupcake and gestured at the dance floor. "Shall we?"

Back on the dance floor, she started showing him a few more moves and pushing up the tempo. He knew the role of teacher left her a bit impatient. She would glance longingly at her friend, the desire to swing apparent on her face.

After a while Donovan just stopped. He heaved breath into his lungs. "Listen, I'm going to sit and watch for a while. Why don't you dance with your friends?"

"I invited you. I can't just abandon you."

"You need to have fun and stop being a teacher." He waved at her as he made his way to the gallery. Besides he wanted another cupcake.

The moment he sat down, a man in a red zoot suit grabbed her by the hand and dragged her onto the floor.

Dancers started moving toward the edges of the floor leaving room for Hendrix and her partner. Suddenly, the man grabbed her waist, tossed her in the air and when she came down she slid between his legs and the dance competition was on.

Watching Hendrix dance was spectacular. She was graceful, light on her feet. She knew moves that made his back ache. And having her take the time to teach him was a compliment. He was sure he would never be as good, but he wanted to try.

He couldn't help comparing her to his ex-wife. Erica had been a working model who was six-foot-one and weighed a hundred pounds dripping wet. She'd made good money modeling for catalogs and fashion websites. But she would have never gone swing dancing. Her hair would have gotten messed up. Erica didn't do many things that would compromise how she looked. Hendrix didn't seem to care.

She looked transported as she and her friend launched into a series of jumps, cartwheels, aerial maneuvers and twists. The woman Donovan had seen Hendrix with when he'd arrived moved onto the floor with her partner and the two teams started dancing together, their moves perfectly synchronized. They were having fun. Donovan's feet tapped along with the music. He was having as much fun watching as dancing.

A strange woman approached him. "Come on. Hendrix got you started—you can't sit here all night watching her." She took his hand and pulled him to his feet. "Let's dance."

Donovan didn't want the evening to end, but it did. He found himself dancing across the parking lot as he approached the hotel's entrance. As he passed his grandmother's RV, the door opened and Miss E. poked her head out. "What are you doing?"

"I went swing dancing tonight."

"Are you're not having a midlife crisis? You're a bit young." She stepped back and gestured him inside.

He half jumped up the steps into the RV. "Why do you ask that?"

"You never try anything new unless it's in the kitchen." She sat down in her recliner. An open book lay upside down on the table next to her. "Did you lose a bet? Why did you go swing dancing?"

"I can be fun." Donovan sat on the sofa.

His grandmother grinned at him. "Of course you can, sweetie."

"It was fun."

"You went out with the cupcake girl, didn't you?"

"Why would you ask me that? I would think you already know."

She gave him a shrewd look. "I know everything, pretty much. I'm still trying to picture you swing dancing. Did you have a good time?"

"I had a great time. Hendrix is so uninhibited on the dance floor." He still marveled at the moves she'd performed with her dance partner. He pictured her sliding across the smooth floor, while her friend danced over her.

"I once loved to swing dance. Went to Atlantic City for a dance competition."

Very little surprised Donovan, but this did. He stared at his grandmother. "Really, Miss E.?"

She stood up and moved toward the storage cabinet behind the driver's chair. She pulled out an album and sat down next to him. He'd never seen this album. When she opened it, her younger face stared back at him from the very first photo. She was in the arms of a strange man and they were half crouched in a dance move.

"Who's the man?"

"That's your granddaddy," she said almost sadly.

She never talked about her husband. All Donovan knew was they he'd left her early on in their marriage with a son to raise all by herself. He'd never come around again, at least not that Donovan knew of.

His grandfather was a handsome man. He could see bits of pieces of Hunter and Scott in the man's face. Even a tiny bit of Kenzie who appeared to have inherited the shape of his eyes.

"That's grandpa?" Donovan didn't even know she had a photo of him. As a child, he'd once asked about

his grandfather, and Miss E. had told him Granddaddy Clive had his troubles. She'd never said one
bad word about him, just let them know that Clive
couldn't be there for them.

"That's Clive. He was a handsome man," she said
with a little sigh.

"What happened to him?"

"I don't know. He's around somewhere, I suppose.
After the divorce, we went our separate ways. But he
could set the dance floor on fire. I think that's why I
fell in love with him."

She stroked the photo tenderly and Donovan noticed that age spots discolored the backs of her hand.
One finger was twisted with arthritis and two more
didn't quite move properly. When had Miss E. gotten
so old? Seventy-eight wasn't old anymore. Not like it
had been fifty years ago.

"You never wanted to remarry?" Donovan said.

She took a deep breath. "I didn't have time. And
I wanted to be independent. I didn't want a man just
to have one. That doesn't mean I didn't have men
around, but once your daddy was grown up and you,
Hunter, Scott and Kenzie landed on my doorstep,
being married didn't seem so important anymore. I
had all of you." Her look was tender as she smiled at
him. She patted his hand. "And now I'm going to have
a great-grandbaby to watch over. I've been fortunate. I
have a wonderful life. And now look, I own a casino."

Donovan paged through the album. Most of the
photos were of him and his siblings at various ages.
But the one photo he truly loved was of his grand-

mother at a picnic watching them fondly. "Can I be you when I grow up?"

"You're already plenty grown-up."

They lapsed into silence as Donovan looked through the album. Miss E. bent her head close to him and when he was done, he closed the album and handed it to her.

"I see," she said, "that food revenues are up."

"Going through all the trash was really smelly and eye-opening."

"You would have eventually figured it all out by yourself, right?"

"I don't have time for eventually. I needed to know now." Hunter's job with the casino was done. He'd finished the spa in the casino and was picking up local jobs around Reno and Lake Tahoe now that he'd closed his office in San Francisco. Scott's job wasn't to make money but to keep everything safe. But Donovan and Kenzie were directly responsible for making money and keeping the machine going. He couldn't afford to fail.

"Donovan, what are you thinking?"

Brought back to the present, he sighed. "Sometimes it's overwhelming. This behemoth…is a business like any other business," she said.

"Yes, but a lot is riding on making the casino a success. A lot of things have to fall into place—the shops, the casino, the extra services like the spa, the entertainment and the food." Always the food. "All these needs to work together to keep the machine running smoothly. Knowing that every little

cog in this machine has to run smoothly is almost
terrifying." And his cog was one of the biggest.

Miss E. slid her hand over his. "Donovan, everything is running smoothly. We have a good general
manager and all the different divisions are slowly
falling into place. Revenue is up 7 percent from this
time last year. And next year will be even more dramatic. We've been filling almost 60 percent of our
rooms and Nina's media campaign is really starting
to show. She has a lot more ideas that are still in the
planning stages."

"Things are running well," Donovan conceded.
"I have to admit, I was getting bored in Paris." The
exciting part was opening the restaurant, coming up
with new ideas for food and watching the restaurant
grow. "Creating food here is a huge challenge. A restaurant has a steady clientele of people who order
the same things time after time, but the casino has
different people all the time and we're competing
against the big conglomerate hotels that have bottomless wells of money."

"Trust me," Miss E. said with a grin, "Reed has
bottomless pools of money."

"And we're going to meet him when?" Reed Watson was his grandmother's partner in the casino/hotel.
Everyone was curious about him.

"Soon. His father is not well and Reed has a lot
on his plate right now. But he knows we'll do the job.
Now, tell me about cupcake girl. Do you like her? I
don't know what I love more, her champagne cake,
the cannolis or her chocolate brownies."

"Hendrix does have a way with creating unusual tastes that work," Donovan said.

"Nina, Lydia and Kenzie think she fabulous. And Nina can hardly wait to see what kind of wedding cake she creates."

"Has anyone discussed that with Manny?" Manny Torres was Nina's father and owned a very popular restaurant in Los Angeles and had already spoken to Donovan regarding the menu for the reception. Donovan had worked out a menu of his own and was now trying to find a happy medium between the two very different palates the wedding guests would bring to the table. He had the feeling Nina was leading toward a buffet that would allow guest to pick and choose what they wanted, but she hadn't made a final decision.

Miss E. chuckled. "Manny Torres said he knows when he's been outbaked. Everything is good with him." She put the album away and sat back down in her recliner. "I'm glad you've found someone to relax with. Swing dancing is going to be good for you. Food is good for the body, but dancing is good for the soul." She picked up her book with a sudden yawn. "It's late. Go to bed."

Donovan kissed her on the cheek and let himself out of the RV. As he closed the door, he heard Miss E.'s cell phone ring. She picked it up and said, "Hello, Jasper. When are you coming back to Reno? I miss you."

Donovan closed the door. For all her comments about men in her life, she had one. He needed to talk to Hunter, Scott and Kenzie. Did they know Miss E.

had a boyfriend? *Boy* was a bit of a misnomer, though. Male friend sounded better.

He headed into the hotel, his thoughts moving furiously.

# Chapter 8

Hendrix stood with one hand on the industrial mixer and the other holding a bowl of flour she was gently spooning into the mixing bowl. She was having a hard time concentrating. Sunday was the busiest time of the week for the restaurant and the one day her desserts usually sold out.

Her mind was not on her baking, but on her date with Donovan. She'd already burned one batch of brownies after setting the oven too high. She couldn't afford to burn a second batch. She set the mixer to run at the right speed and turned to the oven to pull cupcakes out of it. She set them on the worktable to cool before putting them in the refrigerator. She'd planned on a cream cheese icing. The blocks of cream cheese warmed on the counter waiting until the cupcakes were cool enough.

She changed the temperature on the oven for the brownies and went back to the mixer. After pouring the mix into pans and setting them to bake, she sat down for a moment.

Thank heavens she always had extras of everything in the refrigerator. Today looked to be one of those days when she would need them.

The door opened and a tall, unusually slim woman entered. She was beautiful with the kind of razor-sharp cheekbones that surely made men turn to look at her when she walked by. Her skin was smooth and the color of blended mocha. She wore a black designer dress with a contrasting design in cream that probably cost more than Hendrix's monthly salary.

"Hello," she said, her voice laced with a thick British accent. "I'm looking for Donovan Russell."

Hendrix's voice failed her for a second, so stunned was she by the woman's beauty. "Customers aren't allowed in the kitchens."

"I'm not a customer. I'm Erica, his wife." She smiled revealing startling white, perfectly straight teeth.

Hendrix jumped to her feet and tried not to stare. Erica was taller than Hendrix who stood five foot ten in her bare feet. "I thought Donovan was divorced."

"Yes, we are. So technically I'm really not his wife anymore." She glanced around the kitchen, a look of approval on her face. "And you are?"

Does that mean she wants to be his wife again? Hendrix felt out of her element. This classically beautiful woman was so different than the Erica from Hendrix's imagination.

She wiped her hand on her apron and held it out. "I'm Hendrix Beausolie. I'm the pastry chef."

"I can see that and you're about to burn whatever is in the oven."

Hendrix gave a little squeak. She'd forgotten to set the timer again. She ran to the oven and opened it. She rescued her brownies just in time. She set the pans on the worktable to cool. "Donovan's not here yet. He went to the farmer's market this morning." He went there every Sunday morning and talked to the local farmers about supplying produce for the upcoming week. Donovan would craft specials around what was available for the week.

"He still likes to pick out his own beets," Erica said with a sigh. She wandered around the kitchen glaring at the cooling brownies and cupcakes.

"Is that a bad thing?" Hendrix asked. Every chef she knew liked to choose their own veggies, citing the freshness of locally grown produce.

"Doesn't he employ people to do that for him?" Erica sniffed at the brownies, a tiny frown furrowing her brow. "These brownies smell heavenly. What is in them?"

"This and that," Hendrix said. "You know, brownie stuff."

With one eyebrow raised, Erica gave Hendrix a hard, searching look. "You're one of *those* chefs."

"I beg your pardon?" Hendrix was not one to feel

slighted, but this woman had a way of making every word sound like an insult.

"Keeping everything a secret." Erica opened the refrigerator and stood with the door open as she studied the pies, cakes and other goodies Hendrix had cooling.

Hendrix felt herself beginning to relax. She didn't owe this woman any sort of explanation for anything. She didn't work for Erica. She immediately didn't like Erica and wondered what Donovan had seen in her.

"You have a broken temperature gauge," Erica said as she closed the door.

Hendrix sighed. She opened a drawer and pulled out a replacement. What was it about this woman that set her hackles up? Usually Hendrix was easygoing and liked everyone. Well, maybe she was a little jealous, she considered. Erica was so beautiful, so poised, so put together. Everything Hendrix wasn't.

Donovan entered and stopped short at the sight of his ex-wife. He looked stunned.

Erica pranced over to him, air-kissed him on both sides of his face. "Marcel sends his best," she said.

"What are you doing here?"

"I just thought I'd visit and see how people live on this side of the pond. I've never been to the Wild West."

Donovan studied her for a moment. "Have you met Hendrix?"

"We were just getting to know each other," Hendrix said. "She wants to know what's in my brownies."

"You'll have to guess," Donovan said with a half grin, "and you might even be right. At least for today."

Erica tossed a surprised glance at Hendrix. "He doesn't lean over you, checking to make sure every tiny ingredient is correctly measured?"

"No. He trusts me." Hendrix couldn't resist a tiny sense of smugness at the tight expression on Erica's face.

"How sweet of him to let you work without his supervision. He must trust you a great deal."

"I haven't burned his kitchen down yet," Hendrix said, then resisted the urge to clap her hand over her mouth before something really insulting ejected from it.

"Erica," Donovan said, dragging his ex-wife's attention away from Hendrix, "have you had breakfast?"

From her tiny waist, Hendrix doubted she'd eaten in the past three weeks.

"I could go for a cup of coffee," Erica said with an airy wave of one graceful hand.

Donovan opened the door and ushered her out without a backward glance at Hendrix. Hendrix tried not to pout. Like any man, he'd abandoned her at the first sight of a beautiful, glamorous woman. She wanted to scream. Instead, she cut out a brownie for herself and ate it.

Hunter stepped into the kitchen. "Came for our brownie fix. Lydia is craving chocolate this morning and Maya insists on brownies for herself and her school friends." He stopped when he saw her standing stock-still in the center of the room. "What's wrong, Hendrix?"

"I just met Donovan's ex-wife." Even in her own ears, she sounded sour and annoyed. She pulled a plate out of a cabinet and started to carve the brownies into neat even squares.

"Erica," Hunter said in surprise, "the she-beast. She's here? In Reno?"

Hendrix could tell that Erica wasn't one of his favorite people. "What did Donovan see in her?" The words slipped out and Hendrix slapped her hand over her mouth. Really, it wasn't any of her business. She and Donovan were just friends.

"To this day, we have no idea," Hunter said. He leaned against the worktable and sniffed at the cooling brownies. "He just up and married her. We had three days' notice to get to Paris for the wedding and we left the day after. They were married about a year and were divorced just as quickly."

Hendrix pondered over what Hunter had just said. She knew without really knowing for sure that Erica had done something to make Donovan marry her. Erica was a touch too slick, too smooth. And Donovan had most likely acted with some noble intention. She would have to ask him at the appropriate time.

Any sense of feeling inferior to Erica dissipated. She opened packages of cream cheese and dropped the cheese into a mixing bowl. She found it easier to think when her hands were busy.

"Why do you think she's here?" Hendrix asked.

"Who knows? She may just need some paperwork

signed. Though Scott would say she's the harbinger of the apocalypse."

Hendrix bit down on her lip in an attempt to not laugh. Harbinger of the Apocalypse sounded like a strong possibility. But that brought her back to the questions of why Donovan had married Erica in the first place. She ran a dozen different scenarios through her mind and nothing quite fit.

Hunter pulled a plate out of a cabinet and started arranging brownies on it.

"How many brownies are you planning to take?" Hendrix watched him curiously.

"Five for Maya. One for me. One for Lydia. One for me. One for Miss E. One for me. One for Scott. One for me. One for Nina." He paused. "Wait. Nina is trying on wedding dresses today, so I'll eat hers. And then, one for me." He finished piling the brownies on the plate and carefully wrapped them in a piece of foil she handed him.

Hendrix shook her head. She'd just make another batch. If the restaurant ran out of brownies, they would have a riot on their hands. She opened the drawer where she stored her flour and went to the sink for her measuring cups.

"Don't worry about Erica. Whatever she wants, Donovan is not about to give to her."

"It's not personal," she said.

Hunter gave her a sharp look. "Oh. Okay. It's not personal. I understand." He started toward the door, stopped and turned back to take one more brownie.

"Who is that brownie for?" Hendrix asked.

"For the baby."

"The baby hasn't been born yet."

"Then I'll eat it." He waved at her as he left the kitchen.

Hendrix leaned against the worktable shaking her head. Those Russells were professional eaters. She liked that about them.

Donovan got a room for Erica. He sat in a chair watching her unpack. Erica was as beautiful as ever. "You're looking good."

"For going on thirty-five." She raised an eyebrow.

"I can see you had some work done to your face."

"That's not a very gentlemanly thing to say. I will never confirm or deny it." She tilted her head flirtatiously in a way that had once charmed him.

He studied her. "You still look good." A little lift there and a little tuck there, the differences were subtle and someone who knew her only casually wouldn't have noticed. But he'd known her for a long time. "You said you always liked my honesty."

She stopped in the middle of hanging up a dress and looked at him. "Only until you got to be a little too honest."

"What's the difference between being honest and too honest?"

"Honest is telling me I'm beautiful. Too honest is telling me I'm vain." She hung up the dress and went back to her open suitcase.

But she was vain. "The *V* word never left my mouth."

"But it was in your eyes." She opened the dresser and set a pile of T-shirts inside.

"How long are you staying?" he asked, eyeing the pile of underwear she'd just carefully refolded.

She gave him a wide-eyed look. The kind of look that used to make him cave in to her demands. He was surprised he didn't feel anything. Absence had not made his heart grow fonder.

"I'm staying for as long as it takes."

Fear coursed through him like a hot knife. "As long as what takes?"

She turned, facing him, hands on her hips. "To talk you into coming back home."

*Hell, no*, he thought. "You wasted a trip. I'm not going back to Paris. Reno is my home and my grandmother is depending on me to get the food and the restaurants here into shape."

"Your grandmother can hire anybody," she scoffed with a wave of her hands.

"You could also have hired anybody," he said. "This is about family."

"We used to be family," she tossed at him.

"Not anymore."

A hurt look spread across her face. "Donovan…" she pleaded.

"You tricked me into marrying you when you said you were pregnant and knew you weren't. I did what I thought was honorable." Family was important to him. Even though the stigma of being illegitimate wasn't the same as it had been even thirty years ago, he didn't want a child of his to grow up with that label. He'd done what he'd thought was the honorable thing.

She looked crestfallen. "I'm sorry, Donovan. I wanted normal. A normal life, a normal marriage, a normal…everything."

"You didn't need to marry me to have 'normal.'"

She sat down on the bed with a look of exhaustion. "Since you left, the restaurant has gone downhill."

"And I told you to hire Marie Odile Arceneau. But you didn't." He knew why. Erica didn't want another woman around who was as beautiful as she was. Marie Odile was competition. "I'm not going back to Paris, Erica. You need to choose between your ego and the restaurant. You can't have both."

She covered her face with her long, elegant hands. "But our restaurant is your baby."

"The baby grew up and I had no new challenges. And you didn't want me to open a second location." He loved the challenge of setting up something new and maybe different, but Erica's insecurities had kept him from pursuing it. She wanted their life together to be all about her and he couldn't play that part anymore. "Maybe it's time you grew up, too."

During the first few months of their marriage, they'd worked together to get the restaurant off the ground. And then she'd had a pretend miscarriage and something went off inside him. The idea of being a father had really appealed to and excited him. He'd fostered images of teaching his son or daughter to cook, to love food as much as he did. But with the baby no longer a reality, the disappointment of the fake pregnancy ate away at their marriage until he had realized they weren't compatible and never would be. Deep down, Erica had known it, too. They'd continued to run the restaurant together, because despite what she'd done, Erica loved it as much as he did. He hadn't thought she'd be so insecure about taking over completely.

"I don't think I can run the restaurant on my own," Erica said quietly.

"Yes you can." She was so good at dealing with customers, waitstaff, vendors, even government officials, but only as long as everything went right. The moment she hit bumps in the road, she turned into a helpless female waiting for someone else to solve the problem. "I left instructions for you, Erica. I wrote down everything I thought would help you. I know you're nervous, but you can do it."

She pouted. Once he'd thought her little pouts were cute, but not any longer. "Donovan…"

"Who's running the restaurant while you're gone?"

She looked away from him. "Claude."

"So you left Claude to run the restaurant so you could come to Reno and get me." Claude was a good at managing the kitchen but not so much with customers. "You need to go back. You've always managed the dining area well enough. Claude can take care of the kitchen. Get Marie Odile as general manager and you're good to go."

Her shoulders slumped. "But I miss you."

He put his arm around her and gave her hug. "You're

fine, Erica. Please, don't cry. You have a lot more back-bone than you give yourself credit for."

His cell phone rang, the ID read Hendrix. "Dono-van," he answered.

"Boss," she said breathlessly, "a fire in the kitchen."

A second later the fire alarms went off. Donovan raced for the elevator.

Hendrix herded people out of the restaurant. "Stay calm. Head for the nearest exit." Smoke billowed out of the kitchen, coating the ceiling with black oily clouds. A little girl started crying and Hendrix scooped her up and handed her to her mother.

She kept everyone as orderly as she could, shep-herding them to safety before heading back into the restaurant. Donovan raced through the empty restau-rant to the kitchen, Hendrix trailed him. Two waiters and the sous chef held fire extinguishers, spraying foam over the stoves. The fire crackled. More black smoke billowed upward toward the ventilation ducts.

Donovan grabbed a fire extinguisher and joined Hendrix as she battled the flames around the oven. A few seconds later a fireman appeared. "Everyone out," he shouted.

Hendrix grabbed Donovan and pulled him out of the way as the fireman, his own fire extinguisher shooting trails of foam, took over the fight.

Hendrix led Donovan to the parking lot. Guests streamed out the exit doors. The fire department set up a perimeter and directed people past the barriers.

Hendrix held on to Donovan.

"What happened?" he asked as he watched firemen enter the lobby.

"I'm not sure. I was taking my last batch of brownies out of the oven when I heard someone shout 'fire.' I checked the kitchen, saw the fire, called you and began to evacuate."

"I want you to take care of the restaurant and kitchen staff. Make sure everyone is accounted for. I'm going to check on my family. If anyone is missing, text me."

"And I'll let everyone in your family I run into know that you're looking for them."

He nodded absently and walked away.

Hendrix found most of the waitstaff huddled in the shade of a palm tree. The kitchen staff had retreated to a shady area across the street. Hendrix made sure everyone had gotten out safely and were accounted for. She made a list of everyone and let Donovan know they were all safe. She saw Miss E. talking to the fire captain and texted Donovan to let him know where she was.

"What happened?" she asked the kitchen manager when she approached him.

Pablo Gutierrez was a tall, slim man with jet-black hair and gray streaks over each ear. He'd worked in the kitchen for twenty years, working his way up from dishwasher to line cook to manager. "Hell if I know. One minute I'm prepping for the dinner crowd, checking the inventory to make sure I have everything. The next minute I hear a muffled explosion and flames start shooting up to the ceiling from one of the stove burners." He frowned, perplexed.

"That's kind of an odd place for a fire to start." Most kitchen fires started in or around the deep fryers when volatile hot oil was splattered.

Pablo scratched his head. "I don't know. We've never had a fire before. Mr. Jasper runs a clean kitchen, and we had barely received any violations before. But in the month since Miss E. took over we've been cited for more violations than in all the years I've worked here."

"Are you saying this is Donovan's fault? Or Miss E.'s fault?" Hendrix frowned. She knew Donovan worked overtime to keep the kitchen working properly, making sure the fire extinguishers were where they needed to be, the prep areas were sanitized properly, food was stored according to health department guidelines and all appliances worked flawlessly.

He shook his head. "I came in to work a couple months ago and found several of the refrigerators propped open and the temperatures way below standards. The health inspector was standing in front of one of the refrigerators writing a citation for improper temps. He held the door open for almost two minutes and then took the temperature. I've never seen anything like that before. He timed me washing my hands. First time he watched me, he told me I had to wash my hands for fifteen seconds. This last time he cited me for improper hand washing because I didn't spend forty-five seconds washing them. I don't know, but something strange is going on around here." He paused, glancing around. His voice dropped to just above a whisper. "Someone cleaned out our first-aid kits again. Donovan has filled up the first-aid kits six times in the past two weeks. And someone is playing hide-and-seek with the thermometers. And twice now someone has removed the evacuation plans from the display case. All of this seems to happen just before a surprise inspection by the health department."

Hendrix had already started carrying medical supplies herself. The first-aid kit in her kitchen had been empty yesterday. For a change her fire extinguishers were in their slots and she didn't have to tear the kitchen apart looking for them. All these little incidents worried her.

"A lot of people could lose their jobs, if things keep going on like this," Pablo said. "The health department will shut us down. And then where will we be?"

Hendrix said nothing. It was obvious...*someone didn't like Donovan.*

## Chapter 9

Miss E. sat in her recliner, her face tired and worried. Scott and Hunter sat on the bench behind the dining table. Donovan leaned against the tiny counter in Miss E.'s RV. Nina was dealing with the press conference. Lydia would have come but was at a meeting at Maya's school. In the twenty-four hours since the fire, everything was on hold. A number of guests had checked out, the casino was only half full when usually weekends were the best days. And the kitchen was closed.

"What do you guys think is going on?" Miss E. asked quietly.

"I'm not paranoid," Scott said. "You know I like to think the best of people."

Donovan locked glances with Hunter who rolled his eyes.

"Someone," Scott continued, "isn't happy that you own the hotel, Miss E."

"I can't imagine who." Miss E. rubbed her eyes. "Captain Boylan did tell me that the fire looked suspicious."

Scott nodded. "He found the remains of a rag on the stove over a lit burner. He sent the ashes and left-over fibers to the lab for analysis. He thinks the rag was soaked in something. With the odor and scorch patterns, it could be arson."

"What about the security cameras? Didn't you see anything."

Scott shook his head. "The cameras in the kitchen shorted out just before the fire. We appear to still have some security issues."

"Fix it," Miss E. ordered. "How long before we have the kitchen back in operation?"

Donovan glanced at his watch. "I have a meeting with a contractor at four."

Miss E. nodded. "Even if they have to work 24/7, I want that kitchen back open as soon as possible."

"How are we going to handle the cooking?" Hunter asked.

"The diner kitchen is operational and limited for food prep because it's small, but with a little reorganization, we can feed our guests."

"Is there any place we can borrow space to accommodate diners while the main kitchen and dining room are under repair?" Miss E. continued.

"Kenzie's ski shop," Hunter said. "The space is finished, but she hasn't put up the displays or the racks yet. Also, it's right next to the diner. We can move tables and chairs into it and at least feed most of our guests. But room service is canceled for the time being and people aren't going to be happy about that."

"Kenzie is not going to be happy to have her store turned into a dining room when she gets back from Vermont."

"She's not here to veto the idea," Hunter replied.

"She'll understand," Miss E. said. "And it's only temporary."

"Let's do this," Hunter said.

Scott nodded.

It would be tough, but it could be done. He wished his kitchen had been far enough away to avoid the smoke damage. The fire marshal had closed his kitchen, too. He wasn't certain what Hendrix would do, but he'd find a place for her. Going without dessert was going to have even more diners up in arms.

Donovan found Hendrix in his office. She appeared cranky.

"There's nothing wrong with my kitchen…I mean your kitchen," she snapped. "Why did the fire marshal have to close it, too?"

"That's his job?" Donovan stayed out of reach.

"How are we going to feed people?" She turned around.

"The diner kitchen is small, but adequate. It will take work and cooperation, but we can still manage to get meals out. We're temporarily moving the dining room to the empty area Kenzie set aside for the ski shop."

"And what about me?"

Donovan sighed. "You don't need to be on the premises to make your desserts. I was thinking an industrial kitchen."

She shook her head. "I can do the baking at home, it will just take longer. And I'll need some sort of van to transport everything. My VW bug isn't big enough to hold more than a dozen cupcakes."

"Are you sure? I can find something else, something bigger. There are a number of industrial kitchens available. I just need to do some research."

"If I'm going to be out of my comfort zone, then I want to be in my own kitchen which I know is up to code." She glanced around, her eyes sad. "This is so frustrating."

"Rein in the cranky." He put an arm around her and pulled her close. "We'll solve this. This is not an insurmountable problem."

"I know." She leaned her head against him. "What's going on?"

"What do you mean?"

"I know I tend to live in my own little world when I'm baking, but even I can see something is going on. The fire extinguishers, the empty first-aid kits, the broken temperature gauges and the broken mixer? During the years I worked for my grandmother, we had only one mishap. The refrigerator broke down and needed to be replaced. It was twenty years old, but she had equipment even older that kept right on ticking."

Donovan didn't know what to say. "I don't want to use the word *sabotage*, but it feels like it. Scott installed more security cameras and still accidents keep happening. I don't know, Hendrix. I just don't know."

She slid an arm around his neck and kissed him lightly on the cheek. "How do we find out?"

"That's Scott's job. And he will find out." Donovan just wished it would happen quickly.

They walked out into the lobby.

A desk clerk pointed at Hendrix and a man in sweatshirt and jeans walked into Donovan's office. "Hendrix Beausolie?"

"That's me." He handed her a business-sized manila envelope. Hendrix accepted the envelope, frowning. "What is this?"

The man shrugged. "You've been served." He turned on his heel and rushed out the lobby doors.

"Served? What?" Hendrix stared after the man's rushed departure.

Donovan took the envelope from her and opened it, skimming the document. She peered at it, frowning.

"This isn't good," he said.

"What is it?" There was a tremble in her voice and fear in her eyes.

"You're being sued by Susan Baxter-Wilson and Lisa Baxter for theft of proprietary recipes, specifically a champagne cake recipe you developed while employed by Mitzi Baxter of Mitzi's Cake Magic." He read through the second document. "And this is an injunction preventing you from selling champagne cake in any variation."

Hendrix stared at him, her mouth wide open, her eyes glazed with shock. "I don't understand this." She took the papers from him. "They think the champagne cake recipe belongs to them?" Outrage filled her eyes.

He was surprised at how angry she'd become. But then again this lawsuit went to the heart of her and understandably. "I think they're implying you stole the recipe for champagne cake from Mitzi Baxter. I'm not a lawyer, but I think you're going to need one."

"I didn't steal the recipe from anyone. It was my grandmother's. I just improved it. And I can't afford a lawyer."

"Don't worry about a lawyer. The hotel has a lawyer on retainer and we've been named in the lawsuit, as well." He wanted to comfort her, but her coldness gave him hesitation.

She glared at him, waving the documents in the air. "I didn't steal anything." She read the injunction again. "They can do this? They can stop me from doing my job?"

"What we need to do is talk to a lawyer. I don't know how to answer your questions." He ran a hand down her arm in an attempt to soothe her."

"Has this ever happened to you?"

"Every chef in Paris knows how to make coq au vin. If we were to start suing each other over recipes, every restaurant in Paris would be shut down and there would be anarchy." Not that there wasn't a dirty under-the-radar war that went on between chefs, but it was a silent agreement to keep it out of the press and away from the dining public.

"But…but…" She gripped the paper as though planning to tear it in half.

Donovan rescued the documents. "These are official. More than likely this is just a nuisance suit, and I think they are going to have a hard time proving you stole their recipe when I know it never tastes quite the same twice. So you can't make champagne cake. Try something new. Black Forest cake. Red velvet cake. Hell, if you wanted to bake a cake with tequila, you could make it work."

Her big eyes bored into him. "Do you believe…"

Donovan placed his finger gently to her mouth. "I don't believe one word of this. You are the most talented pastry chef I've ever known. You take the most common items and turn them into a celebration of life. Right now, there isn't a thing you can do. Let's just turn this over to the lawyer and get back to doing our jobs." He kissed her on the forehead and took by the hand. "Let's go find Miss E. She always knows what to do."

Hendrix was furious. She slammed cake pans down on her worktable and paced back and forth, unable to concentrate on baking. Lisa and Susan were the worst kind of people—they were parasites expecting everyone else to dance to their tune. She couldn't believe Mitzi, who was wonderful and fun, had raised such mean-spirited women. She had to do something to salvage this mess.

She poured batter into the cake pans and slid them into the oven. Even though she liked chocolate cake, her champagne cake was more open to variations. Her grandmother had given her the original recipe and she'd changed it and molded it into something more modern in flavor. That Lisa and Susie were claiming they owned the recipe absolutely floored her.

Could someone own a recipe? She didn't think so. Recipes were readily available. Restaurants guarded their recipes because many of them had secret ingredients. But champagne cake? She'd done an internet search once, and found over a thousand variations on one simple champagne cake recipe.

The front doorbell rang and she ran down the hall wiping her hands on her apron, conscious of the flour billowing around her.

Miss E. and a strange woman stood on the doorstep.

"This is Vanessa Peabody," Miss E. said. "I keep her on retainer for the Mariposa."

Vanessa Peabody was beautiful with a narrow face surrounded by dark brown hair. Her eyes, the color of Jack Daniel's, were serious. She wore a gray silk pantsuit and yellow blouse and carried a Coach tote. Everything about her was classy. Hendrix was too aware of her quirky retro capri pants and white T-shirt. If this case went to court, Hendrix would have to change how she dressed in order to camouflage her eccentricities.

"May we come in?" Vanessa asked in a calm, serene voice.

Hendrix, aware she'd been staring, stepped back. The two women entered and Hendrix directed them to the back of the house toward the kitchen.

Vanessa sniffed the air. "What smells so wonderful?"

"Just plain, old chocolate cake," Hendrix groused.

"Nothing about Hendrix's cakes are plain," Miss E. explained.

Vanessa set her tote down on the counter and dug out a tablet computer. "I believe one chocolate cake is my fee."

"How about a cake a week for the next year?" Hendrix said. "My choice."

Vanessa's eyes narrowed as she studied Hendrix. "Maybe one a month. And one dessert party when this is all over."

"Done." She loved dessert parties. Just the thought sent her thoughts racing over what she could make.

Vanessa sat on a tall stool. She looked calm and elegant. Hendrix found her anger abating.

Miss E. leaned against the counter, her eyes on the cakes already done and cooling on their racks. "Do you have any brownies?"

"Always," Hendrix said with a laugh. She opened the refrigerator and drew out a pan of brownies which she proceeded to cut into squares. She pulled small white plates out of the cabinet and arranged a brownie on each one. Then she sprinkled powdered sugar over the tops. "What's the plan?"

Vanessa tapped on her tablet computer. "The burden of proof is on Lisa and Susan. As the plaintiffs they have to prove beyond any reasonable doubt that you developed the cake while working at Mitzi's Cake Magic. If they can prove the recipe was a trade secret then they might have a case. Proving something like this is going to be extremely difficult."

"Are you saying I shouldn't be worried?"

"Oh, no. If you get the wrong judge on a bad day, you could still be in trouble. If I do a lousy job, I could have proof signed off by the Supreme Court and we still might lose. And if this ever gets before a jury, juries often vote in favor of the attorney they like the best. Clearly, this is a nuisance suit, but even nuisance suits have ended up in court."

Hendrix felt her shoulders slump. "I have about ten variations I do over and over again, and even then the taste is altered depending on how much of one ingredient is present. Baking isn't an exact science."

Vanessa bit into the brownie, chewed and took another larger bite, an expression of bliss moving across her face. "I have a friend whose husband is a color chemist who has a patent for a gray paint pigment."

"Really?" Hendrix asked, intrigued, even though it sounded dumb. Why patent a color? And what did that mean?

"He develops house paint," Vanessa continued, "and while the color itself isn't patented, the process for making it, including the ingredients and their percentages are."

*Who knew?* Hendrix thought.

"May I have another, please?" Vanessa asked with her best Oliver Twist accent while holding out her plate.

Hendrix set another brownie on the plate and watched as Vanessa studied it.

"She makes darn good brownies," Miss E. said. "Just give them to the judge and you'd win."

"I'll second that," Vanessa said. "All we have to do is prove that you've used it in other places before going to work for Mitzi's Cake Magic."

"My grandmother gave me the original recipe. I don't know where she got it, but I'll call her."

Vanessa made a note on her computer. "You do that and I'll start researching legal precedents for food patenting and information about this recipe's origins."

Hendrix pulled glasses out of the cabinet and set them on the table. She had made sweet tea earlier. She poured the mixture into the glasses.

"Where else have you served this cake besides The Casa de Mariposa?"

Hendrix had to think. "I made it for my friends when I was at UC Davis. I made it for my ex-boyfriend's parents' anniversary party."

"Your ex-boyfriend's parents?"

Hendrix grinned. "They wanted to keep me," she chuckled. "My grandmother still serves one of the variations in her tea shop."

"Okay." Vanessa tapped furiously on her computer. "Any place else?"

"I have a list of private clients. I've served the cake, or some variation or it, to all of them."

"I'll need that list. I have a meeting with Lisa and Susan's lawyer on Friday. If I have enough evidence to show that the cake recipe isn't proprietary, maybe I can convince them to drop the suit."

Hendrix shook her head. "I don't think that's going to happen. Lisa and Susan want to drag me through the mud. They are the most spiteful women I've ever known. They are angry at me because I had a better relationship with their mother than they did." Mitzi had told her once that no matter what she did, her daughters never approved of her. They had blamed her for divorcing their father, and Mitzi refused to tell them that he had left her for another woman that he'd been having an affair with. For some reason, they idolized their father and Mitzi had sadly commented that things like that often happened in a divorce. She'd gone on and made a life for herself, and maybe that was part of the problem. She hadn't looked back no matter how hard her daughters had tried to get her back together with her ex-husband.

Vanessa asked a few more questions and Hendrix answered as honestly as she could. By the time the two women left, she was worn out. She finished her baking, loaded up the van and took everything to the Mariposa.

"Have you ever been to the Reno Food and Wine Festival?" Donovan asked as he helped Hendrix load the wheeled carts. After she'd mentioned it to him, he'd researched the event and found out more about it.

"I've been the first in line," Hendrix said, "for the past four years. Want to go Saturday?"

Donovan nodded. "Sounds like fun."

They wheeled the carts through the delivery bay to the diner kitchen. Once the desserts were stored inside the walk-in refrigerator, Hendrix went into the converted dining room. Diners were few and the food was a bit more basic than usual. One of the diners saw her and immediately asked about her brownies.

"Just unloaded them," she answered.

The diner gave her a thumbs-up and went back to his hamburger.

"This looks like it will work out," she told Donovan.

"The room's a bit small, but we'll make do, for now." Donovan led the way into the old dining room, which had been stripped of everything. "I decided since we're going to be down for a few months, we might as well upgrade all the equipment and repaint. I'm ordering new tables and booths. Lydia, Nina, Miss E and Kenzie told me they were all submitting their ideas on how the dining room should look, and I get to pick the design we'll use tomorrow morning."

She cringed. He was a brave man. She admired that about him. "You sound a little dubious."

"Whichever plan I pick, the other three will be annoyed with me."

Hendrix laughed. "What do you want?"

"What any man wants. Comfortable with no fuss."

She got that. She liked it, too. "Comfortable with no fuss doesn't appeal to the customers you want to attract for a fancy dinner."

"Yeah, but it does make me want to sit down in sweat pants and a beer to watch football." He looked wistful.

She giggled and he shrugged.

A workman was pulling up the carpet. Underneath it the concrete floor was stained from years of dropped food and spilled drinks.

"I've decided on porcelain tile instead of carpet," Donovan explained as he led the way into the kitchen. "Easier to maintain."

The kitchen was a hub of activity. The walk-in refrigerators had been pulled out and sat in the center of the room. A workman tugged at a stove. The mixer that was always breaking down had been set near the rear doors to be carted out.

"How did things go with Vanessa?" he asked leading the way to his office.

"Okay, I guess. The only good thing about this mess is that the burden of proof is on Lisa and Susan. Vanessa thinks things will be just fine. Though she warned me that if it goes to a jury trial, the jurors tends to go with the lawyer they like the most. I can't imagine Susan and Lisa hiring a nice attorney. As for Vanessa, I want to make her cookies."

Donovan chuckled. "Vanessa's like a cat. You pet her, she purrs and the next moment she'd digging her claws into your face."

"That's a bit scary," Hendrix said.

"Be happy she's on your side."

"I am. I trust her." Just as she trusted him, but she

wasn't going to say that. She didn't have the nerve to say it.

There was this awkward moment of silence.

"I'd better get going," Hendrix said. "I have a long list of supplies I need to get from the store room, and I want to get started early on tomorrow's baking."

Donovan nodded. "Meet me here on Saturday morning. The booths open at ten"

"I'll be here at nine." She loved food festivals. She gazed happily at Donovan.

Hendrix waited impatiently for Donovan. She'd arrived early, anxious to get to the event. But she soon found that Donovan was off talking with the construction foreman about a problem they'd encountered when they tried to install one of the new ovens.

She sat in the diner, nursing a cup of coffee. She would have had something else but wanted to keep her appetite for the food. She wore jeans rolled up at the ankle, a Rosie the Riveter T-shirt and a floppy yellow hat that matched her yellow sneakers.

Erica, Donovan's perfectly groomed ex-wife walked into the diner, spotted Hendrix and slid into the booth opposite her. Erica wore white shorts that fit her slender hips to perfection and showed off her long, slender legs. A white silk shirt showed a little more cleavage than necessary, and her bright red enamel necklace and bracelet set could only have come from Paris. Dainty gold sandals that looked almost too fragile to be of any use covered her slim feet. She'd brushed her hair back from her long, aristocratic face and secured it with red enamel barrettes.

"You look ready for adventure. You're certainly not dressed for baking. What's on your agenda today?"

Hendrix tried not to grimace. "Donovan and I are going to the Food and Wine Festival today."

"That sounds exciting." Erica leaned over the edge of the table. "Our first date was something similar in Paris. I just love the smell of all those aromas mingling. Food cooking in the streets, people wandering around sampling everything. It was very romantic."

"That's nice." Hendrix didn't think food was particularly romantic. Food was exciting, meant to be sampled and enjoyed.

"I think I'll come along." Erica smiled at Hendrix. "It's been a long time since I attended a food fair."

"This is more business than pleasure," Hendrix said with a frown.

Erica shrugged. "That's all right."

Donovan entered the diner and walked straight over to Hendrix. A thrill of pleasure filled her.

"Erica."

"You're lovely young protégée here just invited me to come along to the food festival."

Donovan's gaze turned to Hendrix and she shook her head. "I don't think so."

Erica's eyebrows rose. "Excuse me?"

"This is business, Erica. I don't have time to entertain you. If you want to find your own way there, be my guest. But you're not tagging along with me and Hendrix."

Erica's mouth fell open in astonishment. She slid out of the booth and stood, taking a deep breath and looking down at Hendrix as though Donovan's refusal to allow her to tag along was somehow Hendrix's fault.

"Well," Erica said. "I know when I'm not wanted." She turned on her heels and walked out.

Hendrix didn't know what to say. She stared at Donovan.

"You didn't want her to come along?" Donovan said as he sat across of her.

"I didn't say that."

"You were thinking it."

She sipped her coffee, her mind racing for a reply. "My grandmother taught me to be mannerly."

"Trust me. Being polite to Erica accomplishes nothing. She once wrangled an invitation to the Cannes Film Festival. She'd been thinking about a new career as an actress. But then she antagonized one of the board members who had the power of making or breaking any actress. And that was the end of her acting career." He stood and held out his hand. "I'm not ready to be run out of Reno on a rail. You ready for a day of food?"

"I've prepared myself emotionally, spiritually and physically. I'm ready to get my *eat* on." She jumped to her feet and put her hand in his. The touch of his fingers sent a tingle through her. She was ready.

The food festival was held in the parking lot of a large shopping mall. Rows of canopies dotted the area. And even before Donovan parked the car, Hendrix could smell mouthwatering aromas hovering in the air. He paid their entry fee and received a book of coupons to exchange for food samples.

She inhaled, pulling apart different smells: garlic, onion, pepper, vanilla mingled with the sharpness of citrus and barbecue. As they stood at the head of the first row she couldn't decide where to start first. Interspersed with the foods booths were vendors selling products.

"So much food and so little time," she moaned. She wanted to try everything. She walked down the aisle, eyeing each booth critically. The sweet smells of pastries reached her and she stopped so suddenly that Donovan bumped into her.

"What?" Donovan said.

She closed her eyes and sniffed in the yeasty aroma. "Bread."

Donovan grabbed her hand. "This way." Even he sounded excited.

The booth proudly announced its specialty breads. Hendrix stood in front of the display counter and stared. Susan stood behind the counter while Lisa stood in front holding a tray with tiny cookies. The two women glared at her and she stepped back, wanting to avoid any confrontation.

"Is something wrong?" Donovan asked.

She pointed discreetly at the booth. "That's Lisa and Susan, the two women suing me for the champagne cake recipe."

Donovan nodded. Then he walked over to Lisa and

took two cookies and brought them back. Lisa continued to glare at Hendrix, who backed farther away.

Hendrix took one and chewed. "Too much cardamom," she said. "I've told them a hundred times to stop putting so much in the cookies. It obscures the nutty flavor of the almonds."

Donovan took a bite. He nodded in agreement. "Needs a bit of vanilla, too. Just a couple drops to add an underlying taste." He paused to finish the last tiny bite.

Hendrix shrugged. "They never liked me. I'm too weird for them."

"What happened?"

Hendrix gave him a sideways look. She liked that he tried to protect her. It made her feel cared for. Special. Her heart tightened a bit. He really did like her. As much as she liked him. "They took over the bakery after Mitzi's stroke and expected me to be happy with what they were willing to give me. They disrupted my whole baking process and wouldn't let me do what I do best. They wanted to cash in on the cupcake craze and wouldn't listen to me when I told them cupcake sales had already crested and were falling off. They wanted me to just be quiet and not offer opinions. Mitzi and I had always talked about everything."

She turned down another aisle, leaving Lisa and Susan behind.

"Don't let them ruin the day," Donovan urged as he planted his hand on the small of her back. "Let's keep moving."

His touch electrified her. Hendrix wasn't going to

let Lisa's and Susan's anger stop her from enjoying herself with Donovan. She was so happy he'd come with her. She followed Donovan to a booth with an open grill made from a drum. A huge man stood in front of it, watching over barbecued chicken wings. He handed out samples to Donovan and Hendrix. She nibbled the wing. It was amazing. Donovan stopped to talk to the man cooking the wings while she wandered over to another display case with a sign prominently advertising a champagne cake.

"Can I try a sample of your cake?" she asked the woman behind the counter. The woman cut a tiny piece and gave it to her on a small paper napkin.

"What are you eating?" Donovan asked.

"Champagne cake," she said, pointing at the display case. "And it tastes remarkably like my version." She pulled out her phone and took a photo of the cake and the sign in front of it. She took a second photo from farther back displaying the sign for the bakery and sent both photos to Vanessa. "If Lisa and Susan are going to sue me, then they have to sue everybody who makes this cake."

"Do you think they know that?" Donovan said with a grin.

"I don't think they care. If I can prove that the recipe is in general use at other bakers, it undermines what they are trying to do. I'm not going to let them win."

"I don't think they can win," Donovan said. "Let them do their worst—we can afford to keep them in court for years."

Staring into his dark gaze, she had this vision of him as her knight in shining armor. She suddenly became really hot imagining him riding to her rescue.

She laughed, threaded her arm around his and pulled him down to the next booth.

By the end of afternoon, Donovan was stuffed. "I want to go home and unbutton my pants."

Hendrix laughed. "Me, too." They walked slowly toward his car. "I loved every moment of today."

"I've never tried so many different barbecue sauces in my entire life. I'm ordering a couple cases of Daddy Mann's Special Sauce for the hotel."

"I found a spice dealer with some unusual spices."

Donovan opened the door of his car for her. She looked satisfied as she slipped into the hot car. He didn't want the day to end. He wanted to spend more time with her.

"I've always gone by myself before," she said as he started the car. "I have never had this much fun by myself." She gave him a look that indicated she didn't want the day to end, either.

His stomach tightened at the prospect. Could he do this? She was so sweet and soft he knew he could totally get lost in her.

Donovan started the car and hoped the air-conditioning would cool him down. "Since this is my first time, I'm looking forward to some of the other food festivals. I checked and there is usually one every couple months somewhere in Reno or Sparks." He had also enjoyed watching Hendrix eat. No tiny little bites for her. She ate with gusto and seemed determined to try everything. He wondered if everything was like that for her. He suspected it was. Hendrix lived her life by her rules and that was unbelievably sexy. He just wanted to be in her orbit.

When they arrived in front of her house, Hendrix opened her car door. "You coming in?"

Donovan smiled. Heat surrounded him. "I think I will."

She didn't wait for him, instead she walked up the sidewalk and unlocked the door. She threw over her shoulder what she hoped was a come-hither look. She opened the door and stepped inside her cool house and walked straight back to her bedroom. Inside her Victorian white lace and red satin room she kicked off her shoes. Behind her she heard her front door close. Then a few seconds passed before Donovan stood in her bedroom door.

"Hendrix?"

"Yes?"

"Are we going to…" He inclined his head toward her bed.

She smiled and pursed her lips. "Yeah, we are."

His pupils dilated and his beautiful lips parted. Then he smiled. "Just checking."

Hendrix walked over to him and threw her arms around his neck then stood on her tiptoes and kissed him.

Donovan's lips met hers and he drew her against him. Her body burned—his mouth branded her to the

core. His seductive tongue teased hers and he felt so
right in her arms. His body shifted with one hand
sliding down her back to cup her rear end. Hendrix
couldn't help herself. She moaned against his mouth.
She liked that he wanted her badly. As badly as she
wanted him.

His mouth left hers. She felt him reach for her
shirt and it went over her head in a second. Then
he proceeded to kiss her again. Dear God this man
could kiss. What he could do with that mouth had to
be illegal. She took a second and helped him out of
his shirt. And then she felt herself floating and she
landed on her mattress. She watched him reach into
his pocket and retrieve a condom. He placed it between his teeth and then he shimmed out of his jeans
and boxer briefs. She bit her bottom lip at the sight
of his glorious erection as he rolled the condom on.

Hendrix didn't think she could wait any longer.
She worked her pants and bra off as quickly as she
could and sat on the bed waiting. Every look, every
touch of his fingers on her skin sent wild spirals of
sensual magic through her.

He pushed her back on the mattress and put his
knee between hers. He hovered over her as his fingers slipped up her thigh and into her slick heat. She
pushed her legs farther apart as his teasing fingers
explored inside her, sliding deeper and deeper until
the sweet pleasure made her whimper.

A hungry moan escaped her and she had to force
herself not to clamp her legs closed on his magic fingers. Hot tingles of desire worked their way through

her body. The pleasure built and built, until it floated on a tremor of desire so strong she could barely see.

He eased down between her spread legs and slipped inside her. He pushed with deliberate slowness.

"Yes." Hendrix ran her hands down his back. He reached for a nipple and drew it between his teeth, teasing the hard nub with a flick of his tongue. She was going to faint. She hadn't felt like this ever. The anticipation, the passion and the depth of her need filled her.

Donovan began to move inside her. The hot sandalwood scent of his skin drove her crazy. She tightened her legs around his hips pulling herself up to meet each thrust as they grew faster and faster. His lips found the sweet spot behind her ear as he whispered her name over and over again.

Her inner muscles clenched, tightening around him and she knew she was seconds from letting go. She squeezed her eyes shut and wave after wave of ecstasy overtook her, flooding her senses with such exquisite hunger and lust she could barely breathe. Hendrix felt herself tumble over the edge and a second later Donovan joined her with one last powerful thrust. His body grew rigid as he poured himself into her.

She cried out.

For a long moment, she lay beneath him, his hands still gently kneading her breasts. As she slid into sleep, she had only one thought—he was way better than her best cake.

## Chapter 10

Hendrix found herself humming as she puttered around her kitchen. She felt as if she were glowing. Every one of her nerve endings was still on fire from their night of almost continual lovemaking. She had never felt so sated in her life. Not until the wee hours of the morning did they finally fall into a deep sleep with Donovan curled around her, keeping her warm with one hand on her breast and the other holding her close to him.

Donovan had left her just before sunrise with a gentle kiss and smile. She'd had the best day of her life yesterday and the best sex ever. Her body felt alive.

A knock sounded on the back door and it opened before she could gather her wandering thoughts.

"I couldn't wait any longer." Billy Hernandez said as he walked into the kitchen. He took one look at her swollen lips and partially opened eyes and grinned. "Someone had a great night," he said as he sat on the counter, swinging his legs.

"What are you doing here?" His voice brought her back to the present and she looked up from her prep table, remembering that she was making brownies. Wow, this was the first time a man had distracted her from her baking. Donovan Russell was a powerful distraction but a welcome one.

"Couldn't wait. I quit yesterday." He cut a wedge off the piece of cake Hendrix had already cut. He popped a bit of the cake into his mouth and closed his eyes in satisfaction as he chewed. "I didn't think I was ever going to get my cake fix again." He took another bite. "Those two women are hardcore jealous of you. Nothing they are doing is going to get Mitzi's Cake Magic back on its feet."

Hendrix sighed. "Sometimes I wish I could talk to Mitzi."

"You couldn't even if you wanted to. They put your name on a list of people not allowed in to see her. We're all on the list."

"I know." Hendrix sighed and finished measuring chocolate powder into the brownie mixture. She wouldn't have expected anything different from them.

"So here I am. I know you said you'd call, but…" He cut another slice of cake and plopped it on a paper plate.

Hendrix didn't know where he put his food. He was tall and skinny and never seemed to stop eating.

"And what they're doing to you is criminal."

Hendrix agreed. She was still seething with anger over the suit. "I'm going to be angry for a long, long time." She turned the mixer on and reached for the brownie pans, laying them out in a row, ready to receive the batter when it finished mixing.

Billy hopped down from the counter and came to help her measure parchment paper for the bottom of the pans. "Do you think your Mr. Russell will hire me?"

"I will get down on my knees and beg and cry." And after last night, he'd cave. The memory of his lips on hers sent a tingle through her that left her gasping for breath. She hadn't had such earth-shattering sex in her entire life. She realized her hands had paused in what they'd been doing. Heat bloomed across her cheeks. Billy gave her an odd look. She hastily looked away.

The front doorbell chimed.

"I'll get it," Billy said and headed toward the front door.

A minute later Donovan entered the kitchen, eyeing Billy suspiciously. Billy chattered away enthusiastically and after one look at Hendrix the tension drained away from Donovan's face.

"Billy worked with me at Mitzi's. Billy, this is Donovan. Donovan, this is Billy. Donovan, Billy needs a job. Can I hire him? I need an assistant."

Donovan grinned. "Done."

Billy's mouth fell open as he stared at Donovan. "That was easy. Too easy. What's the catch?"

"No catches. I've been thinking about an assistant for Hendrix for a couple of days. My kitchen nearly burned down and right now everything she makes with her magical hands is helping to keep us in business. I'm not messing with the karma goddess or Hendrix. You're hired. Get yourself over to Human Resources first thing tomorrow. I'll let them know you're coming."

"I have a big kitchen with an industrial-size oven and fridge. I can bake at my house, too," Billy added.

Hendrix raised her hand and high-fived Billy. "Baking in our jammies and gettin' paid. Living the dream, my friend, living the dream."

"Not together, right?" Donovan said.

"He's seen me in my Betty Boop pajamas before," Hendrix said with a wicked grin.

Billy stood straight. "I've never seen her out of her Betty Boops." For a second he looked startled. "That didn't sound right, did it? I'm out of here. See you tomorrow, Hendrix, Mr. Russell." He raced through the house like a teenager and the front door slammed after him.

"Ignore him," Hendrix said with a grin. "He's the younger brother I never had."

Donovan pulled her into his arms and kissed her. "Keep it that way."

"Oh. Jealous. I think I like that." She kissed him again. "Thank you."

"For what?"

"For hiring Billy. He couldn't stand his job anymore. Lisa and Susan were making him miserable. If I were a different person, I'd say some truly unkind things about them, but my grandmother would be unhappy with me."

"It can hurt when you don't live up to family expectations," Donovan said.

"I can't imagine Miss E. ever being disappointed in any of you." Hendrix turned off the mixer.

"Scott is the only one who inherited her craftiness." Donovan helped her scoop batter out of the bowl and into the cooking pans. "I think she would have liked it if we'd been better poker players."

Hendrix shook her head. "My grandmother would have liked me to be more of a 'let it go, let it flow' kind of person."

"Your grandmother survives in the food business in San Francisco. That's pretty cutthroat."

"My grandmother survives because she makes a person feel bad if they do anything wrong to her. She has this Catholic nun stare that could put the president of the United States in his place. And there isn't a politician who doesn't miss her when they're on the campaign trail. She knows everybody. She treats everyone with respect and makes sure everybody loves her—one scone at a time. I always thought she should run for office."

She put the brownie pans into the ovens and set the timer. "What did you bring me?" she asked when she turned her attention back to him.

"Catalogs." He handed them to her. "For your

kitchen. We have a five-thirty appointment this afternoon with the sales rep and I want you to pimp out your kitchen."

"Pimp out my kitchen." She grabbed the catalogs with the excitement of a woman who'd just scored some major Tiffany bling. "Anything I want?"

"Anything you want."

She sat down on a stool, her heart racing and her palms sweating. "Would you be embarrassed if I cried like a schoolgirl?"

He laughed. "Not at all."

She opened the first catalog but not before she noticed how pleased he looked with himself. "You're not doing this because of last night, are you?"

He kissed the end of her nose. "I'm doing this because dessert sales have increased 32 percent and my grandmother told me I had to make you happy. Also, she's giving you a display case in the diner just for your baked goods."

She could live with that. "You made me happy last night."

He kissed her on the nose. "Then we are on the right path."

*What was not to like about this man?* "To the promised land."

"Have fun. I have a meeting with the linen people and I'll be back to pick you up at five." He waved as he walked down the hallway and out the front door.

She half waved back even though her gaze was on the open catalog. After paging quickly through all the catalogs, she found her thoughts wandering back to

Mitzi. Mitzi had been her other mother, giving her a place to be herself. She hadn't insisted Hendrix follow recipes making the same boring thing day after day. She'd let Hendrix experiment. Donovan was finally coming to understand Hendrix's way of baking. No, she didn't write things down because she kept them all in her head, but she loved the experimenting, the blending of unexpected flavors and the looks on customers' faces as they allowed the flavors to explode on their taste buds.

Then it hit her, she had picked her path before Donovan and his catalogs came into her life. She had to make a decision. She'd wanted her own bakery so she could be her own person and here she was being given the kitchen of her dreams. She had never expected something like this. In her mind, her job at the hotel had been temporary but it was clear that Donovan wanted to make it permanent.

Last night Donovan had showed another side to his personality. They were so different, so at odds with their cooking styles, yet something worked. She and Donovan were two unexpected flavors that had come together in the most surprising way. How had that happened?

The timer on the oven dinged. She pulled the brownies out of the oven and set them on the worktable to cool.

When she'd first started working for him, she hadn't thought they would ever get along. He was too much of a by-the-book kind of chef. And yet they'd found a common ground despite their differences.

She was happier working with him than she'd been with Mitzi and she loved Mitzi.

*Oh, my goodness.* Did that mean she loved Donovan because she was so much happier? She had to think about that. And right now wasn't the time.

Donovan didn't know what he was doing. He'd never been so deeply attracted to a woman before. Not even Erica. He wanted to impress Hendrix and he liked that she looked at him as if he were a big, sexy, cream-filled cannoli.

He'd never known anyone before who had the same consuming passion for food he did. She was unconventional and eccentric, but she knew how to put a dessert together and seduce people with it. She'd certainly seduced him.

After meeting with the linen people, he walked into the restaurant to the sound of hammering and sawing. He liked the new blues and greens he'd finally decided on with Lydia's help. She certainly knew how to make something unremarkable into something truly classy. The restaurant would be the finest dining experience available.

A crash sounded in the kitchen and he heard Lydia cry out.

"What are you doing?" Lydia's voice rose.

Donovan entered the kitchen to find her standing in the center of the huge room staring at a wall of cabinets. "Those are not the cabinets we chose."

"Ma'am," the construction foreman said, "these are the cabinets that were delivered."

"Don't move. Not one step." Lydia dug her phone out of her pocket. She looked like a bulldog—a very pregnant one.

Donovan had thought to help, but Lydia had the situation completely in control. He backed out of the kitchen to let her deal with it. Nothing he could say or do would help things move along any more quickly.

A hand landed on his shoulder and he found Scott behind him. "I need a minute of your time."

"You got it," Donovan said.

Scott led him to a table against a wall. On the table blueprints had been spread out. "Just wanted to show you what I'm doing with the new camera layout." He pointed to various spots marked with ink. "I rearranged the security cameras to give better coverage in the kitchen areas."

Donovan nodded. He had no idea how his brother could figure these things out, but he was the security expert. "My office, too?"

"Do you really want cameras in your office?"

"Why not?" Donovan asked confused.

"It's your private office and I'm sure you want to do *private things* in your *private office*."

"What do you think I'm going to be doing in my office?" Donovan wasn't good at hiding his feelings, but he tried. The least he could do was protect Hendrix's reputation with the staff.

"A good bodyguard is like a piece of furniture. People forget you're there and do things. Use your imagination, bro."

"Oh." Donovan's imagination was getting a workout. "I think I see. No security cameras in my office. But if we do have them, I should be able to turn them off when I want. Or maybe not. Let's go with none at all." In the heat of the moment, he'd forget to turn them off and Scott and his whole security team would get a front row seat to a very exiting show.

"My suggestion is that we put security cameras in the hallway outside your office and on the door to your office. That way if you do something private in your private office, you won't have an audience." A teasing smile lit his brother's face.

Donovan laughed. "I get the picture." If he wanted to kiss Hendrix he wouldn't be sharing it with the world.

Scott rolled up the blueprints. "I spoke with the fire marshal this morning and he believes the fire wasn't an accident. He thinks the rag was left on the stove deliberately. He interviewed all the staff, and according to my surveillance footage, nobody was near the stove just before the fire broke out. He's tracking down all the delivery people who were on site just prior to the fire."

"A lot of odd people work in the food business. And a lot of normal people, too."

"What are you saying?" Scott asked.

"We've had so many odd things happening. The temperature gauges in the refrigerators have been broken or gone missing so many times, I keep extras locked in my desk. The tampering with the fire extinguishers and the first-aid kits. Someone isn't happy."

"It's almost like someone wants to nitpick this casino to death. Nothing major happened until the fire broke out. And even then, you're still feeding everyone so service wasn't completely disrupted. I think whoever is behind all this can't afford to be out of work."

"But why. What's the purpose behind all these little sneak attacks?"

"All of these issues go on record. That means if anything really major goes down, the health department will have this trail of violations. And maybe they could decide to shut the kitchens down completely."

That sort of made sense. "That would ruin us." Who would come to a hotel like the Mariposa if they didn't have all the services they would expect somewhere else?

"I want to run something by you." Scott's face was set in serious lines. "I'm going to pull all the employment records for the restaurant and kitchen staff for the past two years."

"Why?"

"This is an inside job, I just don't know who the inside person is. And then I'm going to start looking at their financials."

"You can't do that. Isn't that illegal? It won't hold up in court."

"How do you know?" Scott looked surprised.

"I watch cop shows."

"I'm not going to use this information to arrest anyone, just to establish a connection. Once I have that, I'll take the information to one of my new friends at Reno PD. After all, I did get them a tank for their SWAT team."

"You sure know how to make friends and influence people wherever you go, don't you?"

"That's the way I roll, brother." Scott just grinned. He tucked the blueprints under his arm and waved as he walked out the door, bypassing Erica who was entering.

Erica stopped and looked around. "This is a major headache." She gestured at the workman.

"Don't I know it. I appreciate that you always handled this type of stuff."

Erica smiled. "It was never easy."

"What brings you here?"

"Would you like my assistance in dealing with all this?"

"No." Erica never did anything without figuring out what she could get back. She always came with a price.

"In that case, I want one last attempt to talk you into coming back to Paris."

"You already know the answer, Erica. No matter how aggravating all this is, I'm not returning."

"You don't owe your grandmother anything."

Her remark irritated him. Just because she wasn't on good terms with her family didn't mean he wasn't on good terms with his. "You may feel that way, but I don't. She's my grandmother. If I didn't know any better she's been plotting this for years."

"I'm sure Miss E. would be really flattered that you think she's that conniving."

*And so are you*, Donovan thought. She'd lied about being pregnant to get him to marry her. Erica being conniving wasn't the same as Miss E.'s meddling. What Erica did had been for selfish reasons. What Miss E. did was out of love for her grandchildren. The whole idea of finding investors and winning the poker game was just too complicated. Too much could have gone wrong.

"Since I can't you convince how badly I need you in Paris, then I'm heading back," Erica said.

He'd done nothing wrong and wouldn't apologize to her for anything. "My home is here and I'm exactly where I want to be with the people I want to be with."

"Including that cute little pastry chef you have the hots for?"

Donovan just smiled. He wasn't going to let Erica get a rise out of him. Hendrix wasn't any of her business. "She makes things interesting in the kitchen."

"And out?" Erica probed.

"A gentleman never tells." Donovan kissed her on the cheek. "Have a nice flight home."

Erica shrugged. She smiled sweetly and left, just as Lydia walked out of the kitchen, a furious look on her face. She held a clipboard in one hand with a stack of orders clipped to it.

"Do you want know what I just found out?" Her voice was so angry it echoed off the walls.

"Do I want to know because you're pregnant and my brother's wife and you may look as sweet as an apple pie, but you scare me?"

"Donovan Clayton Russell," she said, her hands on her hips, her chin jutting forward belligerently.

*Oh, God.* He braced himself.

She held up her phone. "I just found out that someone impersonating me changed the cabinet order from what I originally gave them."

Donovan frowned. "You need to tell Scott."

"How could anyone think I would pick something so tasteless? If Leon and David were still in town I think they were trying to sabotage me."

For a second Donovan didn't know who she was talking about and then remembered they were her stepsons who'd tried to force her to sign over guardianship of Maya to them. "Someone is trying to disrupt us." But who?

"I'll contact Scott," Donovan said. "You straighten out the order and check with our other suppliers to make sure nothing else has been changed."

Lydia nodded. She gripped her phone while flipping through the stack of papers on the clipboard.

Donovan called his brother and Scott told him to meet him in his office and that he would corral Hunter and Miss E. It was time for an in-depth family powwow.

## Chapter 11

The meeting with the appliance company was the oddest meeting Hendrix had ever been to. When she and Donovan were back in his car, she confronted him.

"What was that all about? You insisted he call me back if anyone calls and tries to change the orders. What the devil is going on?"

He started the SUV and cool air flooded the cabin after a few moments. Donovan looked as though he was struggling to stay calm. "This afternoon the workmen were installing new cabinets in the kitchen and Lydia discovered they were the wrong ones. When she called the supplier, she was told the order had been changed. She started calling other suppliers and discovered someone had called posing as her and changed the order for the new flooring from the cream-colored tile she'd chosen to black. And the order for new ceiling fixtures had also been changed. Lydia's on a rampage. And I don't want the same thing happening to your kitchen."

"Who would do something like this? I don't get it."

"Hunter, Scott, Miss E. and I had a meeting this afternoon to try to figure out who would want to disrupt the repairs. The only person we could think of was the executive chef who quit last September."

"How would he know what to do?"

"Because his sister is a waitress in the diner. No one knew because she's married and has a different last name, but when Scott looked at employee records, he discovered the connection."

"What happens now? You can't fire her. You don't really know for sure if she's informing him of anything. And it may be that she's completely innocent. After all, he is her brother, she would talk to him. And he would know…"

"But that doesn't explain the broken mixer, the broken and missing temperature gauges, the fire extinguishers being hidden in different places and the empty first-aid kits. Someone on the staff has to be behind that."

Hendrix nodded. Evidence was not in favor of the waitress. "What are you planning to do?"

"Keep an eye on her."

Donovan drove Hendrix back to her home. He pulled in behind a strange car parked in the driveway next to her VW bug. When Hendrix exited, the door to the Camry opened and Vanessa Peabody stepped out looking elegant in a pale gray suit with a purple silk blouse that matched the purple stilettos on her feet.

"I've been waiting for you," Vanessa said without preamble. "Also, I'm hungry. Do you have anything to eat?" She followed Donovan and Hendrix to the front door. Hendrix unlocked the door and opened it to the cool interior. She led the way down the hallway to the kitchen where she flipped on the overhead lights.

"You're asking me if I have food?" Hendrix said with a laugh.

"I had to skip lunch." She opened her briefcase and pulled out her tablet and a manila file folder.

"What brings you to visit?" Hendrix hung her purse on a hook inside the pantry, and then pulled out a storage container of mixed crackers she'd made a few days before. From the refrigerator, she removed a round box of Brie cheese, a jar of strawberry jam and another one of jalapeño jam. She popped the Brie into the microwave.

She set plates on the table. While Donovan poured wine into glasses, Hendrix arranged crackers on a round platter with the Brie in the middle and scooped the strawberry and jalapeño jam into round bowls. She set the platter on the table, her mouth watering. Brie on crackers with strawberry jam on top was one of her favorite snacks.

Vanessa turned on her tablet. "Those two women are insane."

"You mean Lisa and Susan?" Hendrix asked, though she already knew.

Vanessa nodded.

"What happened?" Donovan asked as he handed Vanessa a glass of wine.

"Let me preface this by saying there are over 8,348 recipes for champagne cake on the internet. And at least another 1,301 more in various cookbooks. And I know this because I just paid my intern twenty-four dollars an hour to count them and it took her two days. And those are only the English ones." Vanessa held up her glass of wine, looked at it and drained it in one long, extended sip. She held the glass up for more. Donovan obligingly refilled her glass.

"That's all?" Donovan said. He sipped his own wine, his face thoughtful.

"I could have saved you the time." Hendrix said. "I knew approximately how many recipes you would have found." She settled on a stool, spread Brie on a cracker and dropped a dot of strawberry jam on top. She popped it in her mouth.

"I have built into the countersuit that they will have to pay all the legal fees incurred should they lose, assuming this ever gets to court. And as for that shyster lawyer they hired…" Her voice trailed off as she took another sip of wine and bit into a cracker. "I think he found his degree in a trash bin." She poked at her tablet computer. "They have a lot of nerve…" Again her voice trailed away as she stared at her tablet. "They amended the lawsuit and are now asking for twenty million dollars in compensation."

Hendrix sat down, stunned. "Twenty million dollars!"

"Basically, if you give them twenty million dollars tomorrow, they will be happy to drop the lawsuit."

"Yeah," Hendrix said, "let me go open my piggy bank."

"You don't have to pay them anything," Donovan said.

Hendrix chuckled as she held up her hand. "Sarcasm alert."

"Oh," he said, and bit down on his cracker. The Brie oozed over the edges. "This is good." He gave Hendrix a curious look, but she simply shook her head. She'd tell him later what else was in the jams besides strawberries or jalapeños.

"This is totally ridiculous." Vanessa tackled a cracker, chewed it and closed her eyes as though she was being transported to another world. "This is amazing, Hendrix. I love it."

"Thanks," Hendrix said.

"I'm preparing a motion to have this dismissed as a frivolous lawsuit," Vanessa continued.

Hendrix nodded even though a part of her just wanted to go to court and fight. "Somehow this whole thing makes it look like I cheated."

Vanessa patted her hand. "Hendrix, I know how you feel. I want to fight, too, because not only are these women mean, but their lawyer is so shady, I want to do whatever I can to put him out of business. But, the fact of the matter is, this is going to cost money and there are other legal issues way more important than champagne cake that need to come before the judge. There are too many lawyers who waste the court's time when more important issues with serious ramifications need to be taken care of."

Hendrix sipped her wine. Her reputation was at stake, too.

"I can't speak for my grandmother," Donovan said, "but I'm pretty sure she'd be inclined to support the countersuit."

Hendrix held up a hand. "And this is another point. As much as I appreciate your grandmother's confidence in me, I should be fighting this suit. My reputation is being attacked."

Donovan slipped an arm around her and hugged her. "You're part of the Mariposa family now. Lisa and Susan have no idea what the consequences are of taking on the Russell clan. We are smart."

"If their choice of lawyer is any indication, being smart isn't swimming around in those women's gene pool," Vanessa said, grabbing a couple more crackers. "I can't get enough of these crackers. I know chefs don't ordinarily give out their recipes, but would you consider giving it to me?"

"I'd be happy to," Hendrix replied.

"Anything you say to me is confidential." Vanessa looked hopeful.

"I'll give you copies of the jalepeño and strawberry jam recipes. The crackers take too much time—just buy a high-end brand and you'll get the same taste result."

"That's assuming you wrote anything down," Donovan said, teasing gently.

Hendrix laughed. "I don't play with jams too much. I love the interaction of flavors between the salty crackers, the Brie, the sweet strawberry jam and the spicy jalapeño jam."

Vanessa started to pack up her tablet and the file folder. "What do you want to do, Hendrix?"

"I want to drop them off a mountain into an active volcano." Hendrix sipped her wine and put the glass down. "Do whatever you have to do to make them go away." Her reputation might suffer in the short-term, but in the end she would still be the winner. She could develop other cakes. Nothing she baked was dependent on any one recipe.

"Well, I don't think it's ever going to make it to a jury," Vanessa stood, smoothed her skirt over her slim hips and brushed a few wandering crumbs off her blouse. "But to be on the safe side, we'll have to be prepared for that possibility. I better get going."

Hendrix walked her to the front door. "I'll message you the recipes."

"Thank you." Vanessa looked at her for a moment and then reached out and hugged her. "Before I met Miss E., I had the most boring practice in Reno. Now I'm making the world safe for those who love champagne cake." She waved as she walked down the front walk to her Camry.

Hendrix closed the door and leaned back against it, almost too tired to move. She heard the clanging of pans in the kitchen. Smiling, she walked back to the kitchen to find Donovan bent over, searching through her refrigerator.

"I'm making dinner," he announced as he drew an onion, potato, yellow zucchini, red pepper, tomato and carrots out of her refrigerator. "Have you ever had ratatouille? I make a mean one. And you have all the ingredients."

She sat down at the table, and poured herself another glass of wine. And with her chin cupped in her hand, she watched him bustling about her kitchen and thought how comfortable he looked and how comfortable he made her feel.

"Can I help?" she asked.

"Find a wine to go with this. You have a nice little selection in the pantry. I've got the rest."

He gave her a look that just about melted her heart. She grinned at him and went to the pantry to search for a wine to go with their dinner.

Donovan watched Hendrix put the last dish in the dishwasher. Unlike him she was very neat in the kitchen. Funny, he never thought that would be such a turn-on, but something about her flipped his switch.

"You are staring at me." She tilted her head at him.

"You are beautiful." With her face flushed and her hair falling down her back, she was the most alluring woman he'd ever met.

"Your ex is perfect."

"She does look perfect, but a lot of what's inside is fake."

"Then why did you marry to her?"

"At this moment, I have absolutely no idea."

"You are a weird guy, Donovan."

"Maybe." He walked up to her and turned her to face him. Using his body he pushed her against the kitchen countertop until she was not quite sitting on it.

"What are you doing?"

"What do you think?"

"Are we going make love here? In the kitchen?"

"I like your kitchen."

She nodded toward her bedroom. "I have a perfectly good bed in a perfectly good bedroom."

"You have good light and a lot of counter space right here." He reached under her top and pulled it over her head and then unclasped her bra. Her breasts fell free, round and heavy in his hands. He cradled them, his thumbs circling the nipples until they grew hard. She leaned back, resting her hands on the counter, her breasts jutting forward. His breath caught in his throat at the way she posed.

"Like what you see, Donovan Russell?" she purred.

He kissed each breast reverently, his tongue circling the tight nub, and then pulled her legs apart so he could settle between her thighs. His erection was so hard, he was going to burst.

God, her mouth was so soft. Everything about her was soft and sweet. He liked that about her, among so many other things. She smelled like the finest cinnamon and most expensive vanilla.

Their tongues danced together and for a few moments he forgot about all the crazy things going on and focused on the warm desirable woman before him.

He cupped her face and pulled her closer to him. Her hands trailed over his back up to his shoulder and tangled in his hair. She pushed him away enough to fumble with the buttons on his shirt. He leaned farther back to help. When her bare hands touched his skin he thought he would explode.

He reached for her jeans and unsnapped them and tried to work them down her hips. "This isn't working."

"I have a bed in a room." Her eyes were heavy-lidded with passion, her mouth bruised and swollen. She looked wanton and so desirable he started to unbutton his jeans.

"I want you here."

She laughed.

He loved the deep, throaty sound of Hendrix's laugh. It wasn't polite and sweet, but robust, loud and unrestrained. Everything about her was so real. Alive. Passionate. Like her food. Like her personality. She was amazing.

He felt her hands on his stomach sliding down to his pants. The soft rasp of the zipper caught his attention and her fingers slid inside to grasp his erection. His breath caught in his throat. Reaching into his back pocket he pulled out his wallet and quickly pulled out a condom. Then he stepped back and shimmied out of his pants. She twisted until she worked her jeans down her hips to her thighs and then slid them down her calves to puddle on the floor.

"Let me." She took the condom from his trembling hands. Quickly she rolled the latex over the hardness of his penis. The touch of her fingers made him even harder.

Hendrix slid her hips to the very edge of the counter, grabbed his shoulders and moved her legs up and around his hips. Donovan took her hard and fast, thrusting into her tight moistness. His orgasm built to such intensity he could barely keep his balance.

"You feel so good, so…so…" He couldn't find the words.

His tensed and his muscles strained. Deeper. Deeper. She began to tremble, to whimper while urging him deeper.

Her eyes closed. He felt her orgasm build. She tensed. Her inner muscles gripped him so tightly he couldn't stop himself. Suddenly, she screamed. He could feel the spasms of her inner muscles gripping him until he finally let go and climaxed with her. He hung suspended, his body pressed to her, her nipples hard peaks against him.

"You are going to kill me," he said when he finally found his voice.

She laughed and kissed him. "What a way to go."

Yeah, he thought. And he'd go gladly.

## *Chapter 12*

Donovan cracked eggs into a bowl, whipped them and dropped them onto the hot skillet. His favorite breakfast was an egg omelet seasoned with parsley, sweet basil and sage. On the counter a small flat-screen TV blasted out the dulcet tones of their morning host, Toni Aquilar, who shared her observations on the events and happenings in Reno every morning beginning at six.

Donovan stifled a yawn. He'd gotten little sleep and had only left Hendrix's place an hour ago. She'd been elbow-deep in flour and barely even noticed him walk out the door.

"Good morning, Reno," Toni yelled as she walked out onto the sound stage, arms wide. She was a perky looking woman with the trademark blond hair of female TV commentators, a heart-shaped face and a tiny body that made her head appear too big. She wore a too-tight dress that left most of her legs bare and jewelry that was just a tad too flashy to be tasteful. "We have a wonderful show for you this morning. We'll be giving you the inside scoop on what is being labeled the Reno cupcake wars. Don't miss this exposé. Back in four minutes." She kissed the palm of her hand and then blew the kiss at the audience who clapped wildly. The opening credits flashed across the screen and then faded to commercials.

Reno Cupcake Wars! What was that all about?

His omelet sizzled enticingly on the stove. He gently swirled it, added cheese, flipped one half over the other and gently deposited it on his plate. He added more cheese and leaned against the counter, plate in hand.

A few minutes later, Toni Aquilar reappeared sitting on an ivory sofa, legs crossed and a wide smile on her face. "Welcome back, Reno. Today I have with me, Lisa Baxter and her sister, Susan Baxter-Wilson, long-time Reno residents and owners of the bakery, Mitzi's Cake Magic. Please welcome them."

Donovan stared at the TV screen. *What?*

"Ladies," Toni said perkily, "I understand things are brewing at Mitzi's Cake Magic."

"Yes, our mother, Mitzi Baxter trusted a loyal employee with our family recipes who then stole those recipes and quit, taking them with her to her new job at The Casa de Mariposa."

Donovan grabbed the remote, set the program to record and immediately called Miss E. "Turn on your

TV right now. Channel 24." His grandmother turned on her TV and then he heard a gasp.

"Mitzi's Cake Magic has been a fixture in Reno for thirty years," Lisa said with a dramatic wave of her hands. "And in one week, this woman, Hendrix Beausolie, destroyed everything our family has built."

*I need to call Vanessa and then Nina*, Donovan thought. This whole situation is going to need immediate damage control. He speed-dialed Vanessa and when she answered he told her what he'd just told Miss E. He disconnected and called a sleepy-voiced Nina and gave her the same information. Then he called Hendrix, but his call went to voice mail. She was probably baking and didn't have time to answer. He'd have to try again.

"Our mother trusted her with all our family recipes," Susan put in. "And she stole them and is now using them to repair the reputation of that down-and-out casino, Casa de Mariposa. That place should have been torn down years ago. It's an eyesore."

Donovan dropped his plate. It landed safely on the counter, but the fork bounced across the floor. His phone rang. "I know," he said to Scott. "I'm watching it and recording it."

"Good. I'm with Miss E. She's talking with Vanessa Peabody. Nina is trying to call the station and set up an interview to air our side of the story."

"This is a case of big corporations trying to squash family-owned businesses," Susan continued, her face twisted in anger.

"Our mother was so devastated, she had a stroke

and can no longer function. She doesn't even know who we are," Lisa added, her face showing sorrow.

Donovan shook his head. He wasn't hearing this.

"That is so sad," Toni said in sympathy. "I understand you filed a lawsuit."

Lisa nodded. "It's imperative that we protect our family name and our business. If small-business people don't stand up for themselves, then who will?"

Donovan hadn't been angry before, but he was now.

"I hear so many things are going on over there at the Mariposa," Susan added. "The health department is on their case and they recently had a very mysterious fire."

Donovan gripped his phone so tightly his hand began to hurt. He needed to get a hold of Hendrix before she heard about the interview. He called Miss E. and told her where he was going and asked if she could keep an eye on the kitchen.

Before he knew how, he'd arrived at his car, peeled out of the parking lot and was on his way back to Hendrix's house.

Hendrix danced around the kitchen. She'd woken this morning feeling upbeat and happy. Vanessa said everything would work out and Hendrix believed her. The timer on the oven went off and she pulled out the chocolate cakes and set them on the worktable to cool. While butter softened in a mixing bowl in preparation for the icing, she started on her brownies.

She'd decided on double fudge brownies with white chocolate vanilla chips.

Her thoughts drifted to Donovan as she watched the mixer and readjusted the temperature on the ovens. He was the most dynamic man she'd ever known, and the fact that he shared her love of food made her just plain happy. The sex was darn good, too. She licked a bit of batter off her finger. Brownies had always been her comfort food.

The front doorbell chimed. She danced down the hall to answer it to find Donovan standing there. He wore an angry scowl on his face and Hendrix began to tremble. She'd done something and he was furious. Her heart nearly stopped at the fury in his eyes.

"We have to talk." Donovan grabbed her hand and drew her back to the kitchen.

Her mind stuttered. "What's wrong?" He was going to fire her. She closed her eyes and braced herself. She should have known better than to expect anything.

"Lisa and Susan have taken to the airwaves."

Hendrix opened her eyes. "Excuse me?"

"Lisa and Susan were on *Good Morning, Reno* and stated that you stole their mother's secret family recipes and are now using them to repair the restaurant's reputation at the Mariposa."

Hendrix couldn't move. Her brain wrestled with his statement. "I don't understand."

"They've taken the lawsuit to the court of public opinion."

Hendrix sat down, staring at him. "Are you here

to…to fire me?" Her voice trailed away as the enormity of the situation overwhelmed her. Vanessa had promised that everything would be okay.

"God, no," he half shouted. He kissed her, letting his lips tell her his feelings. He then told her about the interview that Susan and Lisa had done this morning.

"This is never going to end, is it?" Tears gathered in her eyes. Donovan and his family had come to mean something to her.

"They're trying to rattle our chain."

"You don't need to fight this battle for me." Hendrix wiped her eyes with the cuff of her jacket.

"We've already had this discussion," Donovan said, his tone indignant. "And now Lisa and Susan have dragged my whole family into it by accusing us of stealing you from Mitzi's Cake Magic and bringing the family secrets along with you."

"Lisa and Susan walked into the bakery, ordered us around and did nothing but criticize us. I brought those recipes to the bakery with me. I developed them long before Mitzi ever hired me. If they could ask her, she'd tell them."

"I'm afraid Lisa and Susan have claimed that your supposed theft caused her stroke."

Her mouth fell open as she glared at him. "What? What?"

His phone rang suddenly. He answered. When he hung up, he said, "That was Vanessa. She wants a family meeting and I'm to bring you."

"I'll call Billy and have him get over here right now." Hendrix was suddenly so angry she could barely talk. She gave Billy an overview of what was going on, and he told her he'd be there in ten minutes.

"How can they lie like this?" she asked.

"They want the big pay day. Twenty million bucks goes a long way." Donovan drew Hendrix into his arms. "We're going to fight this."

Hendrix couldn't let his family do this for her. She was at fault for not taking Lisa and Susan more seriously. If she'd known Lisa and Susan would go to such lengths, she would've just given them the recipes and developed new ones. She'd let her pride get in the way and now the whole Russell family was involved. She had endangered their hotel, their livelihoods and their future.

As Donovan opened the passenger side door to usher her into the SUV, she found herself sinking deeper and deeper into guilt.

The conference room was large and impersonal with gray walls, a teak table large enough to seat twenty people and a sideboard that contained an urn of coffee and a tray with cups.

Miss E. sat at the head of the table, Hunter sat on her right and Lydia next to him. Scott stood in a corner talking on his phone while Nina sat next to Lydia.

Hendrix found a spot as far away from everyone as she could without appearing standoffish. How could they be so nice to her after this disaster?

Vanessa entered, slapped her briefcase on the table and sat down, frowning. "That TV interview Lisa and Susan did is going to make the hotel suffer."

"We need to do some damage control," Nina replied. She tapped her iPad.

"What kind of damage control?" Vanessa asked.

"Unless this interview is picked up nationally, I don't think we have to sweat it," Nina said. "Most of our business is tourism and tourists don't generally watch local news. They don't come to Reno to be mired in reality. These are people on vacation looking for a good time and good food. And if we make a big deal of this, it becomes a big deal. If this case even makes it to trial, we'll let the court handle it. The Casa de Mariposa has been a part of the Reno landscape longer than the bakery. We'll figure it out as we go along."

"You could fire me," Hendrix said.

Silence fell over the room as everyone turned to stare at her.

"Oh, no. Not in this century," Miss E. said. "I will not be bullied by those petty, little spoiled brats."

"But…" Hendrix knew if she weren't around, Lisa and Susan would probably drop the suit. She would give the women her recipes, go somewhere else and develop new ones that bore no resemblance to what she was making now. The more she thought about that option, the sadder she became.

She glanced at Donovan. He wouldn't be in her life anymore. A sharp pain of loss stabbed through her. This man, this hotel, this family had come to mean so much more to her than she had ever thought possible.

Vanessa smiled at Hendrix. "Hendrix, we are fighting this." She glanced around the table. "This is our strategy. If anyone is approached by a reporter, a newspaper, anyone with media ties, your response will be 'no comment.' Let Lisa and Susan spew all they want. This hotel will take the high road. Eventually, Lisa and Susan will say something that will shift popularity away from them. Especially if they spend as much time exploiting this morning's interview as I think they will. *We will remain silent.*" She emphasized the last four words. "So repeat after me—'no comment.'"

Miss E. laughed, but everyone obediently repeated the words. Hendrix added her voice, but her heart wasn't in it. She wanted to track down Lisa and Susan and punch their lights out. And that would be wrong. Her grandma would tell her to "love bomb" them.

The meeting ended soon after. Donovan told Hendrix he would take her home, but he needed to talk to his grandmother for a moment. Hendrix wandered out to the lobby and into the diner.

"We need more brownies," Bonita Diaz, the manager said to Hendrix after she sat down at a table overlooking the lobby. "I'm almost out."

"You'll have them later this afternoon," she said. Billy would deliver them once all the desserts were made.

"I can't believe what I saw on the TV this morning about you." Bonita brought over two cups of coffee and sat down across from Hendrix. "I don't believe any of the accusations. You're an artist. Artists are always original. I've tasted pretty much every brownie in the world—" she patted her hip "—and yours are the best."

"Thank you." As much as Hendrix appreciated her words, they didn't make her feel any better.

"I agree." A woman at the next table turned around. "My name is Lenore Abernathy and I'm totally in love with your brownies. I own a restaurant in New York, and I would kill to have you work for me."

"I don't know," Hendrix said, doubt creeping into her voice. She might want to run away, but she still owed the Russell family her loyalty.

"Just think about it." Lenore handed her a business card. She smiled and stood, stopping at the register to pay her bill.

Hendrix turned the business card over and over. Piquant! Lenore Abernathy owned Piquant! Even Hendrix had heard of the world-famous restaurant. How could she say no to this opportunity? A job in New York might get her out from under this lawsuit. With her gone, Lisa and Susan had no reason to pursue anything.

"You can't go," Bonita said, shaking her head.

"But it would solve everything," Hendrix objected.

Bonita put a hand over Hendrix's. "No. Then those two women would win."

"They're suing the hotel for twenty million dollars. No one should sue for that kind of money over a piece of cake."

"Tell that to Marie Antoinette. A piece of cake started a whole revolution."

Hendrix couldn't help the laugh that escaped her.

"That's not why the revolution happened. I know my history."

"But the myth is so much more fun." Bonita stood and took the empty coffee cups back to the kitchen while Hendrix pondered what to do. She stuffed the card into her pocket.

Donovan appeared in the doorway. "Ready to go?"

Hendrix scrambled to her feet. "Let's go dancing." Dancing was the only thing that could make her feel good right now.

"Okay, I'm in."

# Chapter 13

Hendrix parked her VW behind her grandmother's tea shop. She sat for a moment, breathing in the salt air, listening to the fog horns on the bay, and soaking in the chatter of early-morning tourists. Finally, she opened the car door and stepped out into the chill morning air. In the distance she could hear the barking of sea lions and the sounds of early charters on their way out to sea. How she missed this.

She opened the back door of her grandmother's shop and stepped into the kitchen and immediately reveled in the aromas of cinnamon, vanilla and caramel. The kitchen was empty, but she heard the sounds of her grandmother's laugh coming from the front.

Hendrix loved the tea shop. It was decorated with bright posters on the walls, wood tables and chairs and lots of brightness. She glanced fondly around. Her mother maintained a retail area that looked as though Woodstock threw up in it, only better smelling. Rows of photographs lined one wall showcasing autographed photos of all the celebrities who'd spent time in the shop.

Olivia Prudhomme Beausolie stood behind the register wearing a beautiful yellow-and-white Indian sari threaded with silver. Hendrix's mother had brought it for her from India. Hendrix's mother had brought Olivia clothes from all over the world and Olivia wore them all. Her taste added to the eclectic feel of the shop.

Her grandmother was tall, only an inch shorter than Hendrix. She stood straight, her gray hair in dreads gathered into a bundle down her back. Her face was almost unlined except for the crinkles around her eyes that only showed when she smiled. But she always smiled.

"Hendrix!"

"Hi, Grams," Hendrix said, grabbing an apron from the back of the counter and tying it around her waist. The shop was filled almost to capacity.

"I thought you were coming the weekend after next." Olivia stood back and opened her arms wide.

Hendrix stepped into the embrace, her grandmother's sandalwood perfume enveloping her. "I changed my mind and decided to surprise you."

"And we all know how much I love surprises," Olivia said.

Several customers stood up and rushed to Hendrix. "I miss you, Hendrix," a dainty Chinese matron said.

"Mrs. Li, I miss you, too." Hendrix bent down to kiss the tiny woman on the cheek.

Two uniformed police officers grinned jauntily at Hendrix. "Can I put in an order for your triple chocolate brownies, Hendrix?" one of them said.

Hendrix grabbed a coffeepot and refilled their cups. "Sure. I'll bake some before I head back to Reno." She grinned at them. The two officers had been coming to Hippie, Tea and Me since Hendrix had been a child. The sight of them sitting at the table in the corner always made her feel safe.

"Don't go back to Reno," the other officer said. "Stay here and marry me."

Hendrix paused as if to consider his proposal. "I think your wife would object."

"She loves your fruit tarts too much to make a fuss. I'm sure we can work something out."

Hendrix slid back into the rhythm of the place. She served tea, coffee and pastries while her grandmother disappeared into the kitchen to finish her daily baking.

During a lull after the breakfast rush and just before the afternoon shift arrived, her grandmother brewed a pot of tea and gestured for Hendrix to sit on the other side of the counter. She arranged cookies on a plate and set them in front of Hendrix.

"What's going on?" Olivia asked calmly. No matter how hectic life became, her grandmother sailed through it with a serenity that Hendrix envied.

Hendrix sighed. "Don't get me wrong, I love my job at the Mariposa, but I've brought them nothing but trouble."

Her grandmother rested her fingers on Hendrix's. "Tell me all about it."

The words wouldn't stop. Once she started, Hendrix told her grandmother everything. Starting with Mitzi's stroke and her daughters taking over the bakery to the TV interview and the threat they posed to the Mariposa. "And the worst part is, I think I'm in love with Donovan." She clapped her hand over her mouth. She hadn't meant to say anything about him. The decision to leave Reno made her heart ache.

"Well," Olivia said, a faint frown on her beautiful face. "That's quite an accusation these two women are making. And anybody who knows you knows that your ego is way too big to stoop to stealing."

"Thank you, Grams. I think." Hendrix bit into her grandmother's sugar cinnamon cookies. The taste was exquisite. "I wouldn't be much of a chef if I couldn't develop my own recipes."

Her grandmother smiled. "I remember meeting those two once when I dropped you off after Burning Man last year."

Hendrix remembered that meeting. She shuddered. Burning Man had been the worst two days of her life. No toilets, no shower. Grandma refused to get a hotel room. She did Burning Man old-school.

"They had bad auras," Olivia continued. "I'm surprised they haven't hired a hit man."

"I'm sure if they lose the twenty million dollars, a hit man will be next on their list."

"Sweetie, do you think you might be projecting a little?"

"No." Hendrix shook her head, firmly. "They're crazy. They're not even fun crazy like great-aunt Edna."

Olivia grinned. "I remember when Edna used to stand out in the middle of Haight-Ashbury and belt out show tunes. Those were the days."

Hendrix had always had the opinion that great-aunt Edna was crazy because she'd had a little too much to smoke. She'd always been mellow. Yet Hendrix had really fond memories of her. There hadn't been a mean bone in her body.

"Why are you here? You didn't come all this way to discuss my sister."

Hendrix leaned her elbows on the table. "I was offered a job in New York. I think I should take it. If I leave the hotel, Lisa and Susan might not follow through on the suit. And then I'll write down the three hundred variations on the champagne cake recipe I've worked up and give them to them."

"I doubt that will satisfy them, not when this all hangs on twenty million dollars and the accusation that you stole Mitzi's recipes."

Hendrix covered her face with her hands. "What do I do?"

Her grandmother patted her cheek. "Running away isn't going to help."

"What would you do?"

Olivia raised a clenched fist. "Fight. I didn't raise your mother, and your mother didn't raise you, to give in to the man. You learned from the cradle to fight the bogus system of the oppressors."

Hendrix sipped her tea. "Grandma, this is just a little mom-and-pop bakery. They aren't *the man*."

"When I marched on Washington in 1963…"

Hendrix held up a hand, a tiny laugh erupting. "It's sort of nonsensical talking about champagne cake and the Civil Rights March in the same sentence."

A customer entered. Olivia took a moment to take the man's cookie order, bag it and take his money before returning to Hendrix. Her elbows on the counter, Her chin cradled in her palm.

"Oh, no. It's the same thing. Once you start rolling over on the little things, it's easy to roll over on the big things. You give up your power on this, and you'll give up your power on anything." She pointed a finger at Hendrix. "Mr. Cosgrove…"

"What does my eleventh grade history teacher have to do with anything?"

"Remember the essay you wrote on the Tuskegee airmen and he said there were no black pilots in World War II? I lugged thirty-two books down to the school and threw them on his desk daring him to give you an F on an A+ paper."

Hendrix had been embarrassed, but that was the one defining moment when her grandmother had fought for her. She'd earned that A+ and she wasn't going to let Mr. Cosgrove cheat her out of it. "I know you're right, but this is not just about me, this is about

Miss. E., Donovan and Jasper. They don't have twenty million dollars to throw away on something this stupid."

Her grandmother glared at her with a look so fierce Hendrix shrank back. "Are you going to let them win something *this stupid*?"

Hendrix shook her head.

"Then you go back there and fight. Now tell me about Donovan."

She should have never told Grams about him. She was like a dog with a bone. "Grandma, he's a lousy dancer, but a phenomenal cook. He's the best lover I've ever had and makes me laugh. He just gets me."

Olivia's eyebrows arched. "If he gets you, then why are you afraid he won't back you up against this lawsuit?"

"I'm not afraid he won't, I'm afraid he will. And if we get a judge who sympathizes with small businesses, there's a chance we'll lose. I wanted to be a part of that bakery. Mitzi promised she would sell me half the bakery when she retired. And I saved every penny to make that happen. Her daughters told me no, so I left. They made me feel like I'm nothing, that I'm disposable and unimportant." Suddenly she knew. "Susan and Lisa aren't after me. I'm just the excuse they need to get the twenty million dollars. Maybe I'm barking up the paranoia tree."

"Rule number one," her grandmother said, then lowered her voice to a whisper, "of paranoia is just because you're paranoid, doesn't mean they aren't after you."

Hendrix was just the means to an end—and the end was twenty million dollars. Anger, so great, rose in her. She jumped off the stool. Lisa and Susan were evil. They were just plain evil. "They're not interested in my recipes. They know their business is failing and they're looking for a financial cushion." The Mariposa was that financial cushion. If her reputation ended up being hurt by all this, it would just be a bonus for Lisa and Susan. The high-end food service was a small community. Donovan's reputation would be damaged, as well. She and the casino would be years recovering.

"If you want to take this job," Olivia said, "you have to wait until the lawsuit is settled. If they're willing to stand by you, you need to stand by them."

Hendrix nodded, suddenly anxious to return to Reno. But not just yet. She needed Grams to keep building her up so she could return with a strong fight.

The tiny bell over the door jangled as the lunch customers started crowding in. Olivia's afternoon servers came from the kitchen, tying on aprons and ready to work. Olivia greeted people and quickly seated them. Hendrix washed out the cups she and her grandmother had used and went into the back to begin baking. Her mind reeled with new resolve.

Donovan entered the control room. He glanced around the large room. Several security people sat at different monitors observing action in the casino, the lobby, the pool area and spa, and the parking structure. A low murmur of conversation was the only sound in the room. Scott sat in front of a monitor. He looked up as Donovan crossed the room.

"What is so important that you had to get me out of bed at—" Donovan looked at his watch "—1:34 a.m.?" He stalked over to Scott who was hunched over a monitor in the control room.

"You have a visitor in the kitchen." Scott pointed at the monitor he was watching.

Donovan leaned over his brother's shoulder. A figure dressed in black wandered around the kitchen poking at the new appliances and opening cabinet doors. The figure wore baggy clothes, a hoodie and a scarf over the lower part of the face. Despite the attempt to cover up, he had the feeling it was a woman.

"Do you know who it is?"

Scott pushed back from the desk. "Not yet. Let's go find out." A young woman took his place at the monitor. He inserted an earbud, rambled off something softly and the woman gave him a thumbs-up. Scott led the way out of the control room to the hallway and the service elevators.

"Are you thinking this is the vandal?" Donovan asked.

"I'm certain it's the vandal." The elevator door slid open with a small hissing sound. "I've been working the night shifts to keep an eye on things." He hit the button for the main floor. "I just had a feeling that all those new appliances would be a huge temptation."

In the lobby, Scott led the way through the casino to the restaurant and into the kitchen. It was empty. The intruder had already moved on. Scott tilted his head, listening. Then he gestured to Donovan to follow him down the hall leading to Donovan's office.

Donovan heard a sound coming from his office. Scott raced in. Donovan stood in the doorway listening to the sounds of the struggle. He heard several grunts and a moment later, Scott reappeared tugging a young woman into the hallway.

"Look what I found," Scott said.

Donovan recognized her. Michelle Cruz. She worked in the diner. As Scott had mentioned, her brother had been the executive chef before quitting after an altercation with Manny Torres, Nina's father.

The woman glared at him as Scott dragged her down the hallway despite her struggles. Once she was safely deposited in the interrogation room, Scott went into his office.

"Aren't you going to talk to her?" Donovan asked.

"I'm calling her union rep first. I want this interrogation to be completely legal." He tapped busily on his phone.

Donovan returned to the observation room and waited. The woman tapped her fingers on the table. She looked around, her face composed and calm. She wouldn't be easy to rattle.

A half hour later, Scott entered the room with a small, fussy-looking man in tow.

Michelle looked up and just smiled.

Scott sat down across from her. "So, can you tell me exactly what you were doing in the kitchen at one-thirty in the morning?"

"I want a lawyer." Michelle said as she glanced at the union rep.

The man nodded and dug his phone out of his pocket. He turned away and dialed, spoke briefly and then disconnected.

"All right," Scott said agreeably. "The lawyer is taken care of. But you aren't under arrest. You don't have to say anything. You don't even have to listen to me. But I'm going to talk anyway."

Donovan watched Michelle closely. She looked completely unconcerned.

Scott leaned forward slightly and began telling her about the tampering in the kitchen. "You do realize that these violations could add up to a serious enough situation that the hotel kitchens would be closed down permanently. This would put you and a number of other people out of a job. And with you being the sole source of income in your family…"

She looked up sharply. "How do you know that?"

Scott shrugged. "It's my business to know."

The union rep interrupted, "Are you accusing Miss Cruz of something?"

"I'm just laying my cards on the table," Scott said. "Did you ever stop to think that you might not find another job if you lose this one?"

"Are you saying you could blackball Miss Cruz in the industry?" The union rep frowned at Scott.

"I can't do anything of the sort. But Reno is a small town." Scott sat back waiting. "You have not only jeopardized your job, but the jobs of a hundred and twenty-seven other employees in the restaurant, diner, bars and kitchens. All for your brother's petty revenge, and to this day he has still not gotten another job."

Michelle started to look worried.

"You have two small children," Scott continued, "your mother and your brother to support. How is that going to go for you? Your brother isn't going to take any responsibility for the vandalism. It's all going to be on you."

Donovan cringed. He'd never seen his brother in such an intimidating manner. He understood why Scott was good at what he did.

"I understand he wants revenge. I'm not a nice guy, either. But in his place, I would never involve anyone else who could be hurt. Your brother doesn't give a crap about you. He's not the type of man you should want to help."

She pressed her lips together firmly, though a worried look appeared in her eyes.

A second later, a knock sounded on the door and a man dressed in a black suit, a power tie and a slick haircut entered. He glanced around the room. "I'd like a moment with my client."

Scott nodded as he stood up and left the room. He stepped into the observation room and turned off the audio. "Privileged information." He stepped back out into the hall and gestured for Donovan.

"What are you going to offer her?"

"I'll get her another job in another hotel. She can't stay here."

"What about her brother? What can he be charged with?"

"Conspiracy to commit vandalism and property damage is probably the only thing we could get him on. Even then, assuming we can prove his involvement, he'll just get a tap on the wrist and community service."

The lawyer opened the door. "You can come in."

Donovan followed Scott into the interrogation room. He hung back in the corner watching the proceedings intently.

"My client is willing to cooperate if you'll help her get another job."

Scott nodded. "I'll have another job for her by end of business today."

Michelle nodded. "My brother was very angry when Mr. Torres scolded him. He lost respect from from the other chefs and kitchen staff. All he could do was quit the job. But he couldn't find another one, so he just got angrier and angrier." She paused suddenly looking weary. "I was wrong to make trouble, but I wanted to help him."

"Vandalizing my kitchen doesn't help your brother," Scott said quietly.

Michelle shrugged. Donovan felt sorry for her.

"Family is important. I'm sorry for what I did. I didn't mean for the fire to start. That really was an accident on my part."

The lawyer cleared his throat. "Everything else is just a misdemeanor and won't go anywhere. And even if you got this in front of a judge, he could dismiss everything as a series of minor pranks."

"I can bring charges against her brother for conspiracy to commit property damage."

"Another charge that won't go anywhere." The lawyer waved his hand.

"It would be on his record," Donovan said.

The lawyer glanced at Donovan. "It would, but would that make you feel better?"

"Miss E. would be the better person and walk away," Scott murmured to his brother. "I think we should, too. But," he said to Michelle, "I strongly suggest you talk to your brother, Ms. Cruz. Let him know that we are aware of what he's done, and we'll be suspicious of anything that happens from now on. That should be enough."

Michelle looked relieved. "I'm sorry. I just wanted to be a good sister. Miguel worked hard to get into the position he was in and he felt the loss deeply."

Donovan smiled at her. "I understand. Food service at high levels can be cutthroat. I have a friend in Denver who is looking for a sous chef. I'm willing to give you the contact information. After that, Miguel will have to figure it out for himself."

"Thank you." Tears welled in her eyes. "Thank you. I did not expect such generosity."

"Then we're done here," the lawyer said, standing up.

Michelle stood, as well, and headed to the door. She paused on the threshold and turned back to face Scott. "I heard about the cabinet order and the floor tiles being changed. Just so you know, that wasn't me."

## Chapter 14

Donovan stood in the center of the restaurant. He held a blueprint in one hand while workers brought in the center buffet and started positioning the cases. He was excited. In just a couple more weeks, the restaurant would be back in business.

Lenore Abernathy entered the restaurant, looking around. She looked extremely chic in a black-and-white suit with a vivid purple floral scarf around her neck. "This restaurant is going to be really nice," she said glancing at the blueprint he held. "Your new menu is going to be a hit."

"Thank you." Praise from Lenore Abernathy was always welcome.

"I'm not the least bit surprised," she continued. "You were a star in Paris."

"I hear a *but* in there," Donovan said.

Her eyebrows rose. "The *but* is, if I had my way, you would be doing it all without that exquisite pastry chef of yours."

Donovan felt a lurch in his heart so painful his stomach clenched. "What do you mean?"

"I made her an offer she can't refuse." Lenore waved her hand dramatically. "Hendrix is going to be the toast of New York and you know how hard it is to impress New Yorkers."

Donovan shook his head. "Hendrix accepted a job offer from you?" Hendrix hadn't said a word. Just when he thought their relationship was finally on firm ground now this news came.

"Not yet," Lenore said, "but she will." She glided away after a tiny wave of her hand. "Back to New York."

Donovan was dumbfounded. When was Hendrix planning to tell him about the job offer? Anger rose, slowly at first and then to fever pitch. She'd used him and that hurt.

Suddenly Miss E. approached with a look of concern on her face. "Is everything all right, Donovan?"

"Lenore Abernathy offered Hendrix a job and seems pretty certain she's going to accept it."

Miss E. tilted her head. "Hendrix told you this?"

"Lenore Abernathy told."

"And what does Hendrix have to say?"

"Lenore…"

"All you have is what Lenore Abernathy said."

"Yes, but…"

She shook a finger at him. "You need to talk to Hendrix and get her side. Until you talk to her, you have no idea what is going on."

"Then I'll talk to her." Donovan stormed out of the restaurant. "As soon as she gets back from visiting her grandmother, I'll be talking to her," he said out loud to himself.

Hendrix had barely dropped her suitcase in her bedroom when her phone rang.

"Hendrix, this is Vanessa." She sounded rushed. "I need you see you right away. I'm convening a meeting at the hotel in thirty minutes."

"Tell me it's good news."

"Just get to the hotel."

"I'll be there," Hendrix replied. "And I have something for you, too."

She jumped back in her VW and headed to the hotel, her thoughts churning. Something must have happened. What had Lisa and Susan done now?

Hendrix parked her car and ran through the lobby and into the administrative center of the hotel. When she arrived in the conference room, she saw that everyone was there, including Donovan. She felt her heart soar at the sight of him. She'd missed him the three days she'd been at her grandmother's.

She found a seat and sat down next to Lydia.

"How are you feeling?" Hendrix asked.

"This baby is still a month from being born, and I can barely walk across the room without putting out my back." Hunter leaned over and kissed Lydia before sitting next to her.

Hendrix simply patted Lydia's hand. She couldn't even begin to sympathize.

Across from Hendrix sat a strange man. She wondered who he was. He was tall and slim with wavy chestnut brown hair, intense blue-green eyes and a narrow face. His skin was a pale white as though he seldom went out in the sun. He wore a white polo shirt and had a tablet computer propped up in front of him.

Nina sat next to him, smiling, with Scott next to her. Miss E. sat at the head of the table with Donovan beside her on her right.

Miss E. tapped the table. "Everyone, before we start, I wanted to introduce Reed Watson."

The man stood up. "Hi, everyone. I'm happy to be here."

Miss E. introduced everyone. Reed sat down and smiled at Miss E.

"My granddaughter, Kenzie, won't be here. She's in Paris on business," Miss E. said. "And with that I'll turn this meeting over to Vanessa."

Vanessa stood and went to the head of the table. She held a thick file folder in one hand. "I'm glad everyone is here. I want you to know that I have quite a bit of interesting news." She opened the file removing the stack of papers inside. She started handing them out. "You all have in your hands the deposition of one Margaret Baxter, also known as Mitzi, owner of Mitzi's Cake Magic."

Hendrix frowned as she took the deposition. She

tried to catch Donovan's gaze, but he studied the papers in front of him. He hadn't said a word to her. What was wrong with him? He looked…angry.

Vanessa sat down. "We need to get through all this information because I've arranged for Lisa and Susan to be here in fifteen minutes." She glanced at her watch. "First off, I had the opportunity to speak with Mrs. Baxter and I found out a few very important things."

Hendrix watched Vanessa, fear pulsing through her. She wondered how Vanessa had managed to see Mitzi, let alone communicated with her.

"Mrs. Baxter isn't quite as incapacitated as her daughters would like us to believe. She had a lot to say and the most important thing was that she didn't launch this suit against you, Hendrix. In fact, she didn't even know about it until she saw her daughters on *Good Morning, Reno*. Mrs. Baxter contacted me and when I arrived at the hospital—"

"You got to see her at the hospital?" Hendrix said in surprise. "How did you get in? I was told no one would be allowed to see her unless they were on the list."

Vanessa grinned. "My name isn't on it. And she's no longer in the hospital but in a rehab facility. And I will say that Mrs. Baxter has been quite put out that no one has come to visit her."

"But…"

With her hand held up, Vanessa continued. "Mrs. Baxter didn't know about the list. She had no idea that her daughters had barred everyone from the bakery from visiting her. Even the customers."

Anger rose in Hendrix. Lisa and Susan said their mother's communication had been affected by the stroke and that she was in a coma. They'd lied to her and to everyone else.

"When I arrived to talk to her, I found her lawyer and a court reporter waiting for me. Mrs. Baxter proceeded to tell me that she didn't launch the suit, nor did she authorize it. She also told me, if you read the deposition, that she had every intention of selling half the bakery to Hendrix and she further swore that all the recipes Hendrix used while working for her are original to Hendrix and the bakery has no proprietary interest in them."

"What does this mean?" Hendrix wanted to cry. Mitzi had always supported her and now she knew that Lisa and Susan were not acting in their mother's best interests.

Vanessa looked at her watch. "We'll know in a moment."

Hendrix pulled a magazine out of her purse and handed it to Vanessa. "My grandmother gave me this. It's a magazine from the early 1950s that she found in a used bookstore. She found the recipe for the champagne cake that she passed down to me in it. I guess I don't need it anymore."

"I'm glad you brought the magazine to me. It further proves that this suit is just a malicious piece of nonsense."

"Twenty million dollars is not nonsense," Hendrix said.

"Don't worry," Vanessa said with a reassuring smile.

The door to the conference room opened. Lisa and Susan, followed by their lawyer, entered.

"So," Lisa said, "you're ready to settle." She looked pleased and a bit smug.

Miss E. stood up. "No. We're thinking of suing you for twenty million dollars and a penny."

Lisa's eyes narrowed. "What are you suing us for?"

Ms. E. eyed her. "You've aggravated me."

The lawyer held up a hand. "What's going on here?"

Vanessa handed him Mitzi's deposition. "You need to read this. But the short version is that you don't have a leg to stand on. I had a long meeting with Mitzi Baxter—"

Susan growled. "What were you doing harassing our sick mother?"

Vanessa handed her a deposition. "Your mother contacted me. She isn't quite as ill as you've led people to believe. And she had quite a story to tell. Do you want to hear it?" She pulled a recorder out of her purse. "I recorded it." She tapped the recorder. "I'm giving you the chance to drop your suit. Otherwise the whole world is going to hear about how you not only conspired to manipulate your poor sick mother, using her illness for your own gain, but also how you tried to destroy Hendrix's reputation. Before you say anything, I'm preparing the paper for a countersuit claiming defamation, making false accusations of theft and anything else I can think of just to irritate you."

Lisa's mouth opened, and then snapped close. She glared at her lawyer. "Can she do that?"

He shook his head. "Oh, yeah." He looked up from the document he held. "I would like a moment with my clients." He stood up and gestured at the door. Lisa and Susan followed him, leaving Hendrix and rest of the room stunned into silence.

Hendrix went back to reading the deposition. As she read, a weight fell away from her. The relief from the boulder of worry she'd been carrying around lifted her spirit. She could get back to doing her job. She grinned happily only to find Donovan glaring at her. What was wrong with him?

Miss E. smiled at Hendrix. "You know it's over."

Hendrix shrugged. "My grandmother says nothing is ever over until it's actually over."

The door opened. Lisa and Susan reclaimed their spots at the table while their lawyer remained standing. "Miss Baxter and Mrs. Baxter-Wilson are willing to drop the suit, but…"

Vanessa leaned forward frowning. "You have no *buts* coming. The lawsuit is dead. If you try to pursue this further, you'll be a laughingstock."

The lawyer ignored her.

Lisa took a deep breath. "Can Hendrix bake for us, too?"

"What?" Miss E. said with a fierce scowl.

Lisa shrank back. "We have employees who will lose their jobs."

Miss E. smiled. "I will hire them all personally. You can't have Hendrix back. You should have honored your mother's wishes to sell Hendrix half the bakery. You shouldn't have lied about your mother being in a coma. There are a lot of things you should have considered before you started the smear campaign against this hotel and attempted to humiliate Hendrix. Now I suggest you all graciously exit my property. And if I were Hendrix, I would expect an apology." Miss E. glanced at Hendrix.

Hendrix shook her head. She didn't want an apology from Lisa and Susan. She just wanted them out of her life for good.

The lawyer left without a backward glance at the two sisters who followed, slinking out of the room.

A moment of silence reigned and then Nina started clapping. "This calls for champagne."

Hendrix didn't think it called for anything. Lisa and Susan had suffered a humiliating defeat. And people so roundly whipped had a way of coming back and bringing fresh anger to the situation. She didn't want to think Mitzi's daughters were vindictive, but she had the feeling they were.

She'd lost the dream of owning her own bakery. With the suit settled, she could seriously think about Lenore Abernathy's offer. But did she want to leave Reno? She had a lot of thinking to do.

"We need to talk," Donovan said, interrupting her thoughts.

Hendrix shook her head. She stood up, bracing her hands against the table. She felt out of sorts for some reason. "I need to be by myself for a bit."

"This can't wait," he insisted.

"Yes, it can." She stomped out of the conference room. She owed Miss E. a thank-you, but the only way she really knew how to show her gratitude was to bake something amazing.

Donovan watched Hendrix leave. He'd give her some space.

Miss E. was introducing everyone to Reed Watson again. He shook hands with everyone and after a bit they all trailed out of the conference room leaving Donovan alone.

He wasn't quite certain how he felt. He was angry with Hendrix. He wanted to vent, to tell her she was making a mistake by accepting this job offer. Yet at the same time, he knew how attractive the offer was. Lenore Abernathy had the power, the smarts and the connections to make Hendrix' a household name. In his mind, he visualized packages of baked products in cute boxes appearing in the bakery aisles of every major grocery chain in the United States.

He could understand the allure. He'd wanted the fame and the glamour of operating a five-star restaurant in Paris. Fame was a lot of work. Once he worked himself into the position, he didn't want it anymore.

He glanced at his watch. Only thirty minutes had passed. He'd given Hendrix enough time to process everything. Now he was going to have his say.

* * *

Even before he knocked on her front door, he could smell the sweetness of her baking. The aroma swept around him while he waited for her to answer the door.

Hendrix opened the door and stood with one hand on her hip, head tilted as she studied him. "I asked for some time to be alone."

"I gave you time."

She stepped aside to let him into the house and turned to walk back down the hall without looking to see if he followed. He stepped into the super bright kitchen, alive with the smells of citrus and vanilla. The blades on the industrial mixer rotated. The oven blinked its readiness. A pan of bright pink batter sat on the worktable waiting to be popped into the oven.

Hendrix glanced down into the mixer and nodded in approval at whatever was in the bowl.

"What are you baking?"

"Champagne cake. It's for Miss E. as a thank-you for everything she's done for me."

"You sound like you're going to accept Lenore Abernathy's offer, then."

A look of surprise crossed her face. "Lenore has a lot of connections. She would help me brand myself and help me get started with my own bakery. I would be able to start over without this debacle with Lisa and Susan hanging over my head." She sat down on a stool and looked at him. Unshed tears sparkled in her eyes. "Since I was a child, I've wanted to own my own bakery."

"You can't go. I'm not going to let you."

Her gaze widened. "How are you going to stop me?"

He pulled her into his arms and kissed her, long and deep. "Don't leave me. I love you."

She stared at him, her mouth partially open. "What?"

"I love you." Donovan put all the emotion he could into the words. "I love everything about you from the way you smell, to the way you look, to the way you bake. I love you." He willed her to understand. He searched her face for some understanding, but she simply looked stunned.

"How could you love me? I'm nothing like your ex-wife."

"Erica is my ex-wife for a reason."

She continued to stare at him. "But I'm…" She didn't finish.

"How about almost perfect?" Amusement rose in him, his earlier anger forgotten. "I know how attractive Lenore's offer is. But I love you and I want you to stay here in Reno…with me." After a few seconds he added wistfully, "Please."

"I'm flattered by Ms. Abernathy's offer. I thought that if I left Lisa and Susan would drop the suit."

"You were going to leave so they'd drop the suit?"

She nodded. "I felt so responsible. I put your grandmother and the hotel into an untenable position. If they'd won the suit, you would have come to resent me."

"Never."

She leaned into his embrace. A small sob shook her. She clutched at him as tears spilled down her cheeks. Donovan found a towel and wiped them away leaving a smear of flour across her cheek. He kissed her again.

"I don't understand why you're crying. I feel like I'm a helpless man here."

Her muffled sobs drained away even though her body continued to shake. "Because...because...I love you, too."

Those were the words he wanted to hear. He unbuttoned her jacket and slid it off. He gently unhooked her bra to let her breasts fall free. Gently he ran his thumb and forefinger around each nipple. "Let me show you how much I love you."

"It's the middle of the day," she said, taking his hand in hers. "Just so you know, I already turned the job down."

"Works for me."

# *Epilogue*

The new restaurant at The Casa de Mariposa was bright and well lit with spacious aisles between the tables and booths lining the wall. In the center, the buffet tables practically sagged under the weight of all the food. Hendrix stood in the center of the buffet. She'd gone all out, making every variation of her champagne cake she'd ever developed. She'd made cupcakes, cakes, pies, tarts and the triple fudge brownies everyone loved.

Donovan stood at the door to greet people. The first customers were everyone on the hotel and casino's staff. Once the hotel employees had their fill, the restaurant would open again to the guests and local customers.

A banner hung over the entrance, announcing the

grand reopening. Hotel employees wandered around the buffet tables looking at the food and taking small helpings.

"I intend to come back for more," one of them murmured to her companion before heading to a nearby table.

Donovan glanced at Hendrix and she felt a warm glow spread through her. He looked so handsome in his white chef's suit with his toque on his head. After the party, they planned to go swing dancing and her feet tapped a rhythm in anticipation.

Vanessa approached the dessert table and opened a large tote.

"That is the ugliest tote," Hendrix blurted out. "Usually you have such beautiful purses."

Vanessa grinned as she opened the tote and took out food storage boxes. She opened one and popped cupcakes in it. She opened another and added brownies. "I told my people I'd bring back dessert for them." She put a storage box inside the tote. "As for the tote, Prada doesn't make lunch boxes and I had to bring something for all my ill-gotten gains." She slid tarts into a third storage box.

"Have at it," Hendrix said with a laugh. She noticed people taking dessert first and food second and she felt pleased.

Jasper Biggins grinned at her as he took two cupcakes. His daughter, Luisa, looked as though she'd been sucking on sour lemons. And when her father tried to urge a cupcake on her, she turned and stalked away.

"Sorry," Jasper said sadly. "She may be thirty-six,

but sometimes she acts like she's five. She's just not a happy person anymore."

Hendrix shrugged.

Miss E. stopped to fill a plate, taking a piece of everything Hendrix had to offer. "What is this?"

"My special raspberry white chocolate truffle. I've been wanting to try a candy-like dessert for a while and with my new kitchen…" Her voice trailed off. Her new kitchen was big and beautiful enough to transport her to heaven.

Donovan slid an arm around her. "This has to be better than being on your own."

She popped a truffle into his mouth. As he chewed, his face came alive. "This is everything I didn't know I wanted till I got it."

He kissed her, his lips tasting of white chocolate and raspberry. "What more do you want?"

She thought about that for a second. She wanted to get married and have a baby, but this wasn't the place to say so. "That's something we'll need to discuss later."

Lydia waddled by. Two days past her due date, she looked huge and weary. Hunter steadied her with an arm around her shoulders as she leaned into him. Lydia's daughter, Maya, trotted alongside.

"This baby had better be born soon," Lydia complained as she passed by. "I'm tired of lugging her around."

Hunter laughed.

The new restaurant was so shiny and clean. Every surface sparkled. The employees wandered around talking to each other.

Scott and Nina approached.

"The champagne cake is divine," Nina said. After a glance at Scott, she added, "I know Miss E. asked you to make one for our wedding."

Hendrix's eyebrows rose. "How about sometime next week we meet and you can sample everything."

Nina nodded. She wandered off, hand in hand with Scott.

"We don't have to stay," Donovan said.

She tapped his arm. "You go tell your grandmother we're leaving." She shoved him. "Go on. Go on." Then she grabbed him. "No. No. Stop."

"What do you want?"

She smiled gesturing at the entrance. "We can't leave. I have to introduce you to my parents and my grandmother. They just walked in." She dragged him away from the buffet.

Her parents, Langston and Gloria Beausolie, rushed over to her. Her mother was a tiny, elegant woman with black hair threaded with gray, large brown eyes and a mouth deeply framed by laugh lines. Her father was tall and muscular with his own hair almost completely gray. He grabbed Hendrix and drew her into a bear hug.

"You came," Hendrix cried. "I wasn't certain you'd make it."

She leaned over slightly for her mother to kiss her. Her grandmother just grinned.

"I wouldn't have missed this for the world," her mother said. She handed Hendrix a narrow box. "We knew this would be a big day for you."

"What's this?"

"A little good luck," her father said.

She tore open the box to reveal a bracelet with four leaf clover charms dangling from the links.

"Thank you." She kissed her mother and father.

"All the way from Ireland," her mother said as she wrapped the bracelet around Hendrix's wrist and secured the clasp.

She introduced Donovan to her parents and grandmother. Her father looked Donovan over from head to toe, his dark eyes scrutinizing every detail. "So you're Donovan. Nice to meet you, son."

Donovan looked nervous. "I'm pleased to meet you, too." He glanced at Hendrix who simply smiled.

"This is quite an occasion," Olivia said.

"Hendrix is the one who made this all possible." Donovan put an arm around her.

From the look on her parents' faces, they knew immediately what his possessive gesture meant. Miss E. joined them and Hendrix introduced her. After a moment, Donovan said something into Langston's ear. The man glanced sharply at Donovan and nodded. The two walked off.

"What are they doing?" Hendrix asked.

Miss E. laughed. "He's asking your father's permission to marry you."

Olivia clapped her hands. "How delightfully old-fashioned."

"That's my Donovan," Miss E. said, pride in her eyes.

Heat bloomed on Hendrix's cheeks. "He hasn't asked me, yet."

"He will." Miss E. patted her on the arm. "Just be patient, dear. Donovan always wants to have things perfect."

Hendrix was so happy she thought she'd float away. She leaned toward Miss E. "Just so you know, I'm going to say yes."

"I already knew that, dear." Miss E. grinned at Olivia and Gloria. "Come with me and I'll get you situated in one of the family suites."

Hendrix soared through the rest of the party. As the employees left regular customers began to filter in.

Donovan grabbed Hendrix and pulled her into the lobby. "Can we leave now?"

"Sure," she said, letting him lead her through the main kitchen to her own private kitchen. "I thought you wanted to go swing dancing."

"In a minute." He pulled her into his arms and kissed her soundly. "I've been wanting to do that for hours."

She grinned.

"Cover your eyes," he ordered.

Surprised, Hendrix raised her fingers to her eyes. She heard him rustle about.

"Okay, you can look now," he ordered.

She lowered her hands and stared at him. He stood in front of her, a cupcake in the palm of his cupped hands. The cupcake was lopsided and the icing looked as if it was supposed to resemble a rose, but she wasn't certain.

"Eat it."

She took the cupcake reluctantly.

"Eat carefully, I don't want you to chip a tooth."

Eyes narrowed, Hendrix peeled the paper casing away and carefully took a bite. The cupcake tasted pretty good. She didn't want to reveal how surprised she was. She took another bite and glanced down. A gleam of something metal showed in the crumbly texture of the interior. She pushed a finger into the center and gently pried the ring from the crumbly cake.

She licked the crumbs off the ring. "Who knew diamonds tasted so good?" She held it out. The center diamond was square cut and surrounded by dark blue sapphires. "It's beautiful."

"Will you marry me?" He stumbled a bit on his words.

"Like, yes." She slid the ring on her finger. "Girls like me don't let boys like you run around free-range."

He kissed her. "Promise me you'll make me laugh for the rest of my life."

"Promise me you won't make cupcakes for anyone else but me."

"Done. You realize we're going to have a fabulous life together."

She nodded her head. "It's going to be legendary. So let's get this started and go dancing."

\* \* \* \* \*

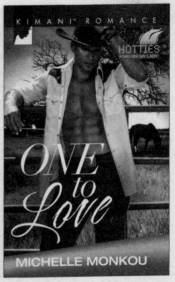

# REQUEST YOUR FREE BOOKS!

## 2 FREE NOVELS PLUS 2 FREE GIFTS!

**KIMANI ROMANCE™**

### Love's ultimate destination!

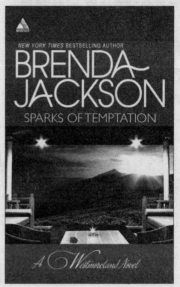